A mysterious menace has finally gone too far

"Here's something for you, Sydney," Ellie said, holding up a cream-colored envelope. "Looks like another RSVP."

Sydney crinkled her forehead in confusion. "It can't be," she said. "All the RSVPs have been in for weeks."

I glanced over as Sydney pulled a thick white card out of the envelope. From where I was sitting it looked just like the response card that had been included with the invitations we'd all received two months earlier. But when Sydney looked at it, her face went even paler than usual.

George saw her expression, too. "What is it, Syd?" she asked.

Sydney turned the card so we could all see it. Just as I'd thought on first glance, it looked exactly like the response cards from Sydney's invitations. But embossed right in the middle of it in fancy script were some extra words:

RSVP: I WILL ATTEN~~D~~
BUT IF YOU
BEST FOR Y

NANCY DREW

Available from Aladdin Paperbacks

KEENE

NANCY DREW

GIRL DETECTIVE®

#36

Aladdin Paperbacks
New York   London   Toronto   Sydney

❧ALADDIN PAPERBACKS
An imprint of Simon & Schuster Children's Publishing Division
1230 Avenue of the Americas, New York, NY 10020
Copyright © 2009 by Simon & Schuster, Inc.
All rights reserved, including the right of
reproduction in whole or in part in any form.
NANCY DREW, NANCY DREW: GIRL DETECTIVE, ALADDIN
PAPERBACKS, and related logo are registered trademarks of Simon & Schuster, Inc.
Manufactured in the United States of America
10 9 8 7 6 5
Library of Congress Control Number 2008930397
ISBN: 978-1-4169-7840-4
0512 OFF

Contents

MODEL CRIME

WEDDING BELLS

"You can stay in the car if you want," Bess Marvin warned George Fayne through the open driver's-side window of my car. "But if you do, I'm telling them to put some extra frilly stuff on your dress."

I laughed as George shot her cousin a disgruntled look and undid her seat belt. Bess and George might be members of the same family, but they couldn't be more different. That's especially true when it comes to clothes. Bess always looks like she just stepped out of the pages of a fashion magazine even when she's only going to the supermarket. George prefers comfort over fashion and would probably wander around town in her pajamas if Bess would let her. As it is, she settles for jeans and sneakers. Me? I'm somewhere in between.

"Come on, we're already late," I said, checking my watch. We'd just found the last parking spot on the block, a few doors down and across Union Street from the River Heights Bridal Boutique. It was Wednesday afternoon, and the leafy commercial block felt sleepy and lazy. The only sign of life was a busy squirrel running up and down the trunk of one of the stately maples that lined the street.

"I told Sydney and Aunt Ellie that I'm allergic to satin, but did anyone care?" George muttered as we all crossed the street. "I still can't believe Syd is insisting I have to be"—she shuddered visibly—"a *bridesmaid*."

"Well, *I* still can't believe Syd is getting married." Bess sighed blissfully. "I remember playing brides with her in our basement when we were all kids."

George nodded, for the first time looking enthusiastic about the conversation. "Never mind that. I can't believe she's getting hitched to Vic Valdez!" she exclaimed. "I can't wait to meet him. He was totally my favorite contestant ever on *Daredevils!*"

Sydney Marvin was Bess and George's cousin. She was a few years older than us, and had moved to New York City when she was sixteen to pursue a modeling career. Now she was coming home to marry her boyfriend of the past year, reality-show contestant Vic Valdez.

I'm not much of a TV viewer, and I'd only watched *Daredevils* a few times. But even I knew about Vic. He'd won his season and turned the show into watercooler fare in the process. The show itself was pretty outrageous, featuring a series of crazy, dangerous stunts at famous landmarks all across the country. But Vic was even more outrageous. His very first week on *Daredevils*, he and the other contestants had been asked to rappel down the side of the Washington Monument using a greased rope to make it extra difficult. Vic had showed up for the task dressed only in his underwear with his entire tall, skinny body painted like the American flag. From then on, more and more viewers tuned in each week to see what he might do next to make the show's crazy stunts even crazier.

Bess kept reminiscing as we wandered across the street. "I always used to change my mind about what sort of wedding I wanted," she said. "Sometimes it was an intimate ceremony on the beach somewhere, and other times I decided I wanted something super glamorous and dressy. But Syd's fantasy never varied. She always said she wanted a small, tasteful, traditional wedding right here in River Heights with all her family and friends."

"Hmm. Well, she stuck to at least one part of that," George commented. "It's going to be in River Heights. As for the rest . . ."

I chuckled. "Yeah," I agreed. "Having a top-rated TV show film you marrying your reality-star man isn't exactly what most people would call traditional."

Bess shook her head. "I still can't believe Syd agreed to that."

"Sounds like she didn't have much choice," George said. "It was part of the compromise they worked out. If she got to have the wedding here instead of in New York, Vic got to have the filming thing."

"Yeah, I know." Bess shrugged. "I just can't believe she went for that. And I *really* can't believe Aunt Ellie was willing to go along with it."

"Sydney told me that Vic thinks doing it will help land him the cohosting gig on the next season of *Daredevils*," George said. "I guess they both want to help him succeed."

By then we'd reached the bridal shop. A little bell over the door tinkled as we entered, and four people looked up immediately. One of them was the owner of the shop. Another, tall and willowy with a head of flaming red hair, separated herself from the rest and rushed over.

"Nancy Drew!" she cried, giving me a hug. "It's

great to see you. Thanks so much for agreeing to be in my wedding!"

"Thanks for asking me, Syd," I replied as I hugged her back. I'd known Sydney forever, of course, seeing that she was the cousin of my two best friends. She'd even babysat me occasionally when I was little. But the two of us had become closer about a year earlier when she'd come back to town so my father could do some work for her. I was fuzzy on the details of said work—I know better than to ask Dad to violate attorney-client privilege, even for something boring like modeling contracts or whatever—but Sydney had spent a lot of time at our house during that time. That was when we'd bonded over our shared love for old black-and-white detective movies. Now, nobody who knows me would be the least bit surprised that I'd have that kind of interest. I'm known around town as a pretty good amateur sleuth myself.

But I was a little surprised when Sydney told me the way I'd solved my latest case reminded her of something out of the *Thin Man* series. That had led to a conversation about our favorite movies—and then numerous evenings spent with a bowl of popcorn in front of one classic film after another, from *The Maltese Falcon* to *The Hound of the Baskervilles*.

It had been great to reconnect with her that way. After she went back to New York we'd kept in touch via phone and e-mail, trading tips on films and also just chatting about life in general. It had been a nice surprise when she'd asked me to be in her wedding party along with Bess and George and a few others.

Now here she was in the flesh. She looked just as great as ever. She was always complaining about being too short for the modeling industry, but at five foot ten she seemed plenty tall to me. Her bright red hair flowed over her slim shoulders, looking extra bright against her pale complexion and the creamy white of the wedding gown she was wearing. Her expression was blissfully happy, which I was glad to see, given all the compromises she'd had to make on her dream wedding.

"Hey, what are we, chopped liver?" George complained as she and Bess watched my reunion with Sydney.

Sydney laughed. "Come on, I saw you two last night at dinner," she said, reaching out to hug George and Bess as well. "I haven't seen Nancy for ages." She turned and gestured toward the other women. "You remember my mom, right, Nancy?"

"Of course she does. Nancy and I are on the Mahoney Foundation committee together." Ellie Marvin bustled over and gave me a hug. Briskly efficient, with sharp green eyes and close-cropped salt-and-pepper hair, Ellie was a familiar figure around town. She was the type of person who knows everyone and gets involved in everything, from raising money for local charities to helping plan the annual Anvil Day parade.

Sydney waved over the remaining member of her little group, a young woman about her own age. She was short and stout, with dark hair and round, red cheeks. I was pretty sure I'd seen her around town, though I couldn't place her until Sydney introduced her.

"This is Deb Camden," Sydney said. "Deb and I have been friends since high school. She's one of the other bridesmaids."

"Sure, I know who you are." Deb giggled as I shook her hand. "Nancy Drew, right? You're always in the newspaper for solving crimes and stuff."

"Nice to meet you, Deb." Her identity had just clicked into place in my mind. "You work at the convenience store over on State Avenue, right? I think I've seen you there a few times."

"Yeah, that was me." Deb giggled again. I was starting to get the feeling she giggled a lot. "I'm working there part-time to help pay my way through school."

"Oh, are you at the University?" George asked. "Uncle Ted teaches there—Syd's dad."

Deb shook her head. "I'm taking classes at River County Community College. I'd have to get at least ten part-time jobs to afford RHU!"

Before we could continue the conversation, Ellie Marvin checked her watch and cleared her throat. "Let's keep things moving, girls. Sydney and I still have to stop in at the print shop after this to check on the programs."

She sounded a little stressed. I wasn't surprised. Thanks to the TV people's schedule, Sydney and her family really hadn't had much time to pull this wedding together. The bridal shower was that Saturday, and the wedding itself would take place one week later.

Sydney sighed, casting one last glance at her reflection in the big mirrors that lined the walls of the shop's main room. "Mom's right," she said. "You know, I'm really looking forward to walking down the aisle and marrying the man of my dreams." She smiled. "But I have to admit, I'm also looking forward to having this wedding behind us and relaxing on the beach in the Caribbean for our honeymoon—with no cameras in sight!"

At Ellie's last comment the bridal shop owner had hurried over to a rack behind the counter. Now she bustled back toward us bearing several plastic-draped dresses on hangers.

"Here you go, girls," she said. "Your names are pinned to the dresses to let you know whose dress is whose. Ready to try them on?"

"We can't wait," Bess told her, shooting George the slightest of smirks. "Right, girls?"

George emitted a groan. "Are you sure you don't want me to, like, work the lights or the sound or something instead?" she asked Sydney.

Sydney laughed. "You're going to look great, George," she said. "Just pretend you're doing my job—I have to wear clothes I don't really like all the time!"

"She's just being cranky," Bess said. "The dresses you picked out are gorgeous—it's obvious you're a fashion pro!"

"Hey, it runs in the family, right?" Sydney replied with a wink.

"Well, *part* of the family, anyway," Bess agreed, sneaking another sly look at George.

I chuckled at George's disgruntled expression. "Come on," I said, reaching for one of the dresses. "Let's get George into the dressing room before she makes a break for it."

The bridal shop owner handed over the dresses. "Now, these just came back from the tailors this morning, girls, so watch out for pins—I haven't had a chance to check them." She shook her head in amazement. "I still can't believe we were able to get the alterations done so fast."

"It's amazing what TV money can make happen,

isn't it?" Ellie commented with a slight roll of her eyes. She didn't sound too happy, which didn't surprise me. Ellie Marvin likes being in charge of things. It had to be killing her to plan her only daughter's wedding on someone else's schedule.

"The bridesmaids' dressing room is right over there," the bridal shop woman said, pointing toward an arched doorway on one side of the counter.

"I'll be there in a minute," Deb said. "I want to help Syd with her dress first."

"Thanks," Sydney said, heading toward a matching doorway on the opposite side of the counter. Her mother and Deb followed, each of them carrying one corner of the long train of her dress.

Bess, George, and I headed into our dressing room, which turned out to be roughly the size of my bedroom at home. Soon all three of us were twirling in our bridesmaid dresses in front of the full-length mirrors. Well, okay, Bess and I were twirling. George was sort of standing there glumly. I guess the sight of herself wrapped in rose-colored satin had sent her into shock.

"I can't believe I'm going to make my TV debut looking like a giant tube of strawberry frosting," she muttered.

Bess shot her a glance. "You look great," she said. "Besides, we probably won't actually be on TV. I think they're planning to use the footage on their website, and then include some kind of *Daredevils* wedding spectacular–type thing on the next set of DVD releases."

"Whatever," George said. "Either way, I—"

She didn't get to finish whatever she was going to say. Because at that moment, from the other side of the shop came a bloodcurdling scream!

RSVP

"That sounded like Sydney!" I exclaimed. "Come on, let's see what's wrong!" We all gathered up our skirts and raced out of the dressing room. Sydney and the others were in the bride's dressing room. Sydney was still in her dress, which was now half-unzipped. She was holding a PDA, staring down at it with a look of horror on her face.

"What's wrong?" Bess demanded breathlessly. "We heard you scream."

"Yeah," George put in. "Did you catch your skin in your zipper or something? I've done that before—it really hurts."

"Nothing like that," Ellie said. "Sydney just received

an upsetting message on her little phone machine."

I hid a smile. Ellie kept on top of most things, but it seemed current technology might not be one of her areas of expertise.

"It's about one of the dresses," Deb explained to us.

Sydney nodded, still staring down at the PDA, which was encased in a stylish green beaded skin. "I just got an e-mail from Akinyi."

"That's her maid of honor," Bess told me before I could ask. "She's a model—she does those cool new perfume ads that are in all the magazines right now. She goes by the one name—Akinyi. Kind of cool, huh?"

"She's my best friend in New York," Sydney said. "We started out together at the agency. She's been my roommate since, like, the first week I came to the city."

I had no idea which ads Bess meant, and I'd never heard of Akinyi. Then again, I'd never heard of most of the high-fashion models Bess could name off the top of her head. But I figured it didn't matter. "So what's the problem?" I asked.

Sydney's lower lip trembled with consternation. "She's doing a shoot in Bermuda this week, so we had her dress shipped out there so she could try it on."

"That's right," the bridal shop owner put in. "We

sent all three of the out-of-town dresses via overnight delivery."

"I told Akinyi to let me know as soon as she tried hers on," Sydney went on. "She's super tall and thin, even for a model, so her dress needed a lot more alterations than the others."

"So what happened?" Bess asked. "It didn't fit?"

Sydney's lip started trembling more than ever. "See for yourself!"

She held out her PDA. The three of us crowded around for a look. The screen was pretty small, but even so it was easy to see the image of a very tall, very thin young woman with gleaming ebony skin and a regal, exotic look. She was wearing a rose-colored dress that matched the ones we had on.

Bess gasped. "Oh, no!" she cried.

I'm no fashion expert, but even I could see why Sydney was so upset. Akinyi's dress didn't fit her at all. It was way too short, for one thing, plus it sagged in several spots where it should have been fitted.

"Akinyi's totally freaking out," Sydney said anxiously. "And no wonder. I mean, the wedding's only, like, a week and a half away, and she's in Bermuda, and—"

"It'll be okay, Syd." Deb put one plump arm around her and gave her a hug. "Really, don't have a cow, okay? We'll work it out."

"Listen to Deb," Ellie added. "We'll take care of this."

The bridal shop woman looked frantic. "It has to be some sort of mix-up," she muttered, pulling a cell phone out of her pocket. "The measurements were right, I know they were. Let me just call that nice woman at the modeling agency who was supposed to forward the dresses. . . ."

I was sympathetic to the problem, especially since Sydney was clearly on the verge of tears. But it didn't seem like there was much we could do to help. So I decided the best thing might be to get out of the way and let them sort it out.

"The good news is, ours fit fine," I told Ellie. "Should we take them with us today?"

"Yes, go ahead, Nancy." Ellie sounded a bit distracted. "Thanks so much for coming out today."

"No problem, Aunt Ellie," Bess said, obviously thinking along the same lines I was. "Maybe we'll see you later, okay?"

Leaving the others dealing with the Great Dress Disaster, the three of us hurried back to our dressing room to change. Minutes later the little bell over the door dinged again as we left the bridal shop carrying our dresses. Actually, Bess was carrying all three of them. She didn't seem to trust George and me to get ours from the shop to the car without ruining them.

We'd barely stepped outside when I spotted some-one rushing toward us. It was Deirdre Shannon. As usual she was dressed in an expensive-looking designer outfit, not a single strand of her long, curly, dark hair out of place.

"Hi, you guys!" Deirdre greeted us with a big smile on her face. "Ooh, are those your dresses for the Marvin-Valdez wedding? They're gorgeous!"

None of us answered her for a second, because we were all too startled. Despite how she was acting at the moment, Deirdre wasn't exactly a close friend of ours. We'd all been in school together our whole lives, so we knew her pretty well—well enough to know that she's a huge snob who thinks most people aren't worthy to breathe the same air she does. At least that's how George likes to put it. Bess and I aren't crazy about Deirdre either, but she *really* rubs George the wrong way.

"Um, thanks," Bess said at last. That's Bess for you. Her impeccable manners can overcome even the most surprising obstacles. "How are you, Deirdre?"

"Great!" Deirdre replied happily. "By the way, did you hear? I'll be at the wedding too."

"You will?" George said. "Why?"

Okay, maybe it wasn't the most polite question in the world. But it was a fair one. As far as I knew, Deirdre and Sydney didn't even know each other.

If Deirdre was annoyed by George's blunt question, she hid it well. "It's a funny story, actually," she said. "Daddy went to law school with one of the attorneys who drew up the releases and whatever other paperwork for this particular, er, project. The attorney called him from LA to check something about our local ordinances or whatever, and I guess the TV people were sooo grateful for his help that Vic Valdez invited our whole family to the wedding."

That was typical. Mr. Shannon is a successful local attorney; he has a reputation for winning his cases no matter what it takes, which means he's always got lots of clients. Deirdre has been taking advantage of his money and connections her whole life.

Her gaze wandered once again toward the dresses Bess was holding. Then she glanced at George, and I braced myself. Deirdre loves to take every opportunity to mock George for her tomboy ways.

"That dress is going to look great on you, George," she said.

"Wha—huh?" George replied, as stunned as I was by Deirdre's compliment. She narrowed her eyes, clearly waiting for the punch line.

Deirdre reached over and fingered the hem of satin fabric sticking out of the protective plastic. "You've got dark hair just like I do, and I know this particular shade of rose works really well on me," Deirdre said.

"I mean, okay, maybe your skin is kind of, you know, swarthier or whatever. And of course, your figure . . . Well, anyway, it should work just fine," she finished brightly.

"Is that supposed to be some kind of—" George started hotly.

She was interrupted by the shrill ring of a cell phone. Deirdre reached into her designer handbag, pulled out her phone, and checked the screen.

"Oops, I'd better take this," she said, pressing the Talk button. "Toodles, guys! See you at the wedding, if not before!"

With that, she pressed the phone to her ear and hurried off down the block. We all stared after her.

"Was that some kind of threat?" Bess joked weakly. "About seeing us before the wedding, I mean."

George rolled her eyes. "Probably just means she's going to try to weasel her way into some of the prewedding events Syd was talking about last night. Just like she managed to weasel herself into an invitation." She frowned. "Anyway, it's totally obvious why she's being so sickeningly-sweet to us all of a sudden. She probably thinks hanging out with the bridesmaids will get her more screen time. I guess she thinks we're too stupid to remember we're not all BFFs."

"Hey, at least she's acting human for a change,"

Bess said with a grin. "Let's not overanalyze it—we should just enjoy it!"

"True," I agreed. "Because it probably won't last long."

We were all still laughing about that when we heard the bridal shop's bell tinkle again. Glancing over my shoulder, I saw Deb Camden hurry out.

"Oh, gosh, you guys are still here!" she said with a breathless giggle. "Wow, stuff is really crazy in there!"

"You mean about the dress?" Bess said. "Did they get that straightened out?"

Deb nodded vigorously, then pushed her straight brown bangs out of her eyes. "They called Syd's modeling agency in New York. The lady there swore she sent them out to the two models just like she was supposed to. But then she checked around and called back, and it turns out Akinyi got sent the wrong dress. Hers is still in New York, and the one she got was meant for one of the other bridesmaids, Candy Kaine."

"Huh?" George blinked. "Candy Kaine? Is that a person, or, like, a holiday treat?"

Deb giggled. "It's the name of another model from Syd's agency."

"I've heard of Candy Kaine," Bess put in. "I think her real first name is something else, like Christy or Connie. But she's got bright red hair like Syd's, plus she's pretty tall and skinny, so some photographer started calling her Candy Kaine and it kind of stuck."

"Oh wait, I remember her," George said. "She's the other redhead in that photo Aunt Ellie and Uncle Ted have framed on the mantel in their den, right? Syd's first big paying job as a model or something?"

Bess nodded. "An ad campaign hired the two of them to play sisters because of the hair thing. I guess they've been friends ever since."

"Anyway, the dresses are being overnighted back to the right bridesmaids as we speak, so they should have them before they get on the plane to come here tomorrow afternoon," Deb continued. "Whew! Syd's so relieved that she isn't even mad at the agency, even though it was their mistake." She shrugged. "It's weird, though. The lady at the agency insists she definitely addressed the right dresses to the right girls." She turned and smiled at me. "I guess it's a real mystery, huh? Maybe you should investigate, Nancy!"

I forced a smile. *Yeah, some mystery!* "Maybe I should," I joked back politely.

Just then Sydney and her mother emerged from the shop. "Oh good, you guys are still here!" Sydney said when she spotted us. "Mom just called the printers, and they won't be ready for us until tomorrow morning. So I was thinking we could all head back to my place and hang out—you know, catch up before all the New York and Hollywood people arrive tomorrow."

"Are you sure?" Bess said. "I mean, of course we'd be happy to help out if there's stuff we can do to help you get ready for the wedding or anything, but we definitely don't want to cause more work by coming over—"

"No, no, I really want you guys to come," Sydney broke in earnestly. "It'll be nice to spend one last afternoon with some normal people."

Her mother raised an eyebrow. "Is this your way of telling me all your friends from New York are abnormal?"

Sydney laughed. "You know what I mean, Mom. I'm just talking about hanging with some regular, down-to-earth River Heights people. Once the TV crew gets here tomorrow, things are probably going to be pretty crazy."

Deb shivered. "I can't even imagine it!" she exclaimed. "I've never been on TV before."

"Trust me, it's not that exciting after a while," Sydney told her with a slight grimace. "But come on-please say you guys will come!"

What could we say? Soon we were all walking into Sydney's parents' house. They lived in a tidy Colonial on Grant Street. Sydney's father wasn't home—he taught Latin at the university and had office hours on Wednesday afternoons. So the house was dark and quiet when we entered.

Ellie had stopped to pick up the mail on her way in. Now she flipped through it as we all headed into the living room. "Here's something for you, Sydney," she said, holding up a cream-colored envelope. "Looks like another RSVP."

Sydney crinkled her forehead in confusion. "It can't be," she said. "All the RSVPs have been in for weeks."

"That's what I thought. But now I'm wondering if someone fell through the cracks somehow." Ellie shrugged. "Maybe your Great-Uncle Farley decided to come back early from Australia."

"Maybe." Sydney took the envelope and slit it open with one pale pink fingernail.

Meanwhile George had flopped down on a cushy armchair, while Bess and I made ourselves comfortable on the sofa in front of the fireplace. Deb was wandering along the mantel, checking out the framed family photos there.

I glanced over as Sydney pulled a thick white card out of the envelope. From where I was sitting it looked just like the response card that had been included with the invitations we'd all received two months earlier. But when Sydney looked at it, her face went even paler than usual.

George saw her expression too. "What is it, Syd?" she asked.

Sydney turned the card so we could all see it. Just as I'd thought on first glance, it looked exactly like the response cards from Sydney's invitations. But embossed right in the middle of it in fancy script were some extra words:

RSVP: I WILL ATTEND.
BUT IF YOU KNOW WHAT'S BEST
FOR YOU, SYDNEY, YOU *WON'T*.

MEET AND GREET

I sat up straight. "Who's it from?" I asked, getting a tingle from my Sleuth-O-Meter—that's what George sometimes calls the weird little sixth sense that tells me when there's a mystery afoot. "Is there a return address?"

Ellie grabbed the envelope from her daughter and checked. "Nothing," she said grimly. "Just a New York City postmark."

"Oh, dear!" Deb's hands fluttered at her cheeks as she stared at Sydney. "I always thought New York seemed so scary. . . ."

Ignoring her, I hurried over for a better look at the RSVP card. Even close up, it was barely distinguishable from the real thing.

"It has the same border I picked out for mine, and the same font, too," Sydney said, her voice shaking a little. "I wonder . . ."

"What?" I shot her a sharp look, instantly noting an odd twinge in her voice. "Sydney, is there something else? Have you gotten other mysterious messages like this in the mail?"

"Not in the mail," Sydney replied. "Um, but I did get a few weird e-mails a week or two ago."

My Sleuth-O-Meter was right. Suddenly it was looking like there might be some kind of mystery here. "E-mails?" I echoed. "What kind of e-mails?"

"They were horrible." Sydney shuddered. "They all said I shouldn't marry Vic if I knew what was good for me, or something like that. Like a threat, even though they didn't really say anything too specific."

"Who were they from?" I asked.

"A bunch of made-up fake addresses," Sydney replied. "The police checked them out and said they were all sent from public computers at libraries or coffeehouses all around New York City. They never figured out who sent them, but I was starting to think . . . Well, never mind. That's all over anyway."

"Why didn't you tell me about these e-mails, Sydney?" Ellie demanded, rushing over and grasping her daughter by the arm. "I had no idea!"

"It wasn't that big a deal, Mom." Sydney sighed and shook her arm loose. "Probably just some of Vic's more obnoxious admirers pulling a prank or something. He's got some pretty weird fans out there."

Ellie still looked horrified. I was a little surprised by that, since she'd never struck me as the type to get so easily rattled. But I was more concerned about getting to the bottom of what Sydney was telling me—and whether it had any connection to the fake RSVP card.

"Do you still have those e-mails?" I asked her. "If so, I'd love to take a look."

"No, I don't have them anymore," Sydney said. "I forwarded them to the police, of course. But then it was like I couldn't think about anything else while they were on my computer. Akinyi and I were both freaking out and couldn't sleep while we knew they were there, sort of like they were haunting us. So she talked me into just deleting them."

I was disappointed. If there truly was a mystery here, it would be helpful to get a look at those e-mails. Maybe I'd be able to guess whether the same person had written them and the RSVP.

Still, it didn't take a detective to figure out that the NYPD was unlikely to just hand over a piece of evidence to a total stranger from several states away. I would have to rely on Sydney's memory of what they'd said.

Unfortunately, she didn't seem too eager to dredge up those memories. "Like I told you, they were all sort of vaguely threatening," she said when I pressed her for details. "You know—'Vic might seem like the one, but he's not the one for you. Add it up before you regret it.' Something like that. I don't really remember the rest that well."

"What do you think it means, Nancy?" Deb asked. "Is it a real mystery?"

"I don't know," I said. "But if it is, I'll do my best to get to the bottom of it."

By the time I met up again with Bess and George the next day, my new case—if that's what it was—hadn't gone much further than that. My friends seemed to think it was nothing to worry about. "Celebrities get weird messages from weird fans all the time," George pointed out as we drove through town. "Those e-mails probably came from some lonely twelve-year-old boy somewhere."

"And what about that RSVP card?" I asked, leaning forward from the backseat of George's car. "It can't be a coincidence that it matches the real ones from her invitations. A random kid wouldn't even know what the invites looked like."

George just shrugged. "Who knows? Maybe it's one of the *Daredevils* guys playing a prank or something."

"Maybe." I'd thought of that possibility myself. During Vic's season, the *Daredevils* cast was infamous for constantly trying to play pranks on one another. Maybe this was their weird way of inducting Sydney into their fraternity or something. If so, it didn't seem like a very funny prank to me, but then again, I'd never really gotten the whole *Daredevils* phenomenon in the first place. In any case, I was determined to keep an eye on things from now until the wedding, just in case there was something more serious going on.

Bess checked her watch. "We'd better hurry," she said to George, who was driving. "We're supposed to be at the airport in less than ten minutes."

"I still don't get why Vic and those guys are bothering to fly in to the River Heights Municipal Airport," George said. "I mean, couldn't they have just driven down from Chicago like the TV people did?"

The *Daredevils* TV crew had descended on the town early that morning, arriving in a long line of vans and SUVs. Half the population of River Heights had turned out to see them drive into town as if it was some kind of parade. At least that was what Dad had told me when he'd called from his office, amused by the whole spectacle. Now my friends and I—along with everyone else involved with the wedding—were on our way to welcome the arrival of the real stars of the show. Namely, Vic and his showbiz pals. After the meet and greet, we were all supposed to attend some kind of welcome party at the airport. They'd told us the dress was "stylish casual." For Bess, that translated into a pair of silky black pants, chic heels, and a shimmery blue top. I was a bit more understated, in nice slacks, a button-down shirt, and flats. George had refused to do more than put on black jeans instead of her usual blue, and dig out her cleanest sneakers.

"I guess they want to film them making a big entrance," Bess said. "Anyway, Syd says the TV people want lots of people there to cheer and stuff."

"Sounds kind of silly to me," I commented.

George shot me a look in the rearview mirror. "What do you know? You hardly ever even watch reality TV."

I couldn't argue with her there. Besides, we were already turning into the small municipal airport, which appeared to be as busy as O'Hare at the moment. There were even a couple of security guards at the entrance gate. They flagged us down and demanded to see photo ID before they'd let us pass.

"Guess they don't want the local riffraff coming in," George commented once we'd finally satisfied the guards that we were who we said we were. "I hope Mom remembered her ID when she came over."

George's mother runs a catering company. Not only was she catering the wedding itself, but Sydney had arranged for her to cater several functions for the TV producers as well. All the extra work was keeping Mrs. Fayne and her employees pretty busy.

"I feel kind of bad about your mom," I told George. "If we weren't bridesmaids, she probably would've drafted all three of us as cater waiters."

George shrugged, not looking too broken up about that. "It's okay," she said. "The TV people are paying her a ton. She can afford to hire all the waitstaff she needs without using us as her indentured servants."

She parked her car and we climbed out. "Which way do we go?" Bess wondered.

"Mystery solved." I pointed to a large man carrying a heavy-looking camera on his shoulder. He was hurrying down a path leading around the side of the main airport building.

We trailed along behind him. When we rounded the back corner of the building, we spotted a crowd gathered along the edge of one of the airstrips.

"Looks like this is the place," George said.

The airstrip was a zoo. Tons of people were buzzing around setting up lights, cameras, microphones, and all sorts of other equipment. About two dozen more familiar faces—Sydney's family and friends—were clustered nearby, watching it all.

We wandered over and found Deb standing at the edge of the crowd of onlookers. "Isn't this exciting?" she gushed, clasping her hands together. Her brown eyes were wide with amazement as she watched a grizzled-looking man stride past, barking orders into a walkie-talkie. "It's like we're on the set of a Hollywood movie!"

"Hard to believe our little Syd is part of this world now, huh?" George said with a grin.

"Hello, hello!" A skinny young man with horn-rimmed glasses and a mop of sandy brown hair hurried toward us. He was carrying a clipboard and wore a large nametag that identified him as Donald Hibbard. "Are you with the bride?"

"Uh-huh. Bridesmaids," Bess said. She gave him our names.

"Wonderful." Donald checked us off on his clipboard. "I'm Donald, one of the PAs. Mr. Eberhart wants me to make sure everyone's here and pass out the releases for you all to sign."

"Mr. Eberhart?" Bess echoed.

"PA?" Deb added curiously.

"Mr. Eberhart is Hans Eberhart, the director," George said before Donald could answer. "He's a genius! I can't believe I'm going to meet him. Is he here yet?" She glanced around eagerly.

"PA stands for production assistant," I told Deb.

"That's someone whose job it is to sort of keep things running on a movie or TV set by looking after all the details." I turned to smile at Donald. "Did I get that right?"

"Absolutely," Donald agreed, returning my smile. He showed us the releases, which basically gave the TV crew the right to use our images in their production. Then he waited while we all signed. "And now I'd better skedaddle," he said, tucking the releases at the back of his clipboard. "I see some more newly arrived details right over there. Enjoy the day, ladies!" He gave us a wave and turned to leave.

But he'd barely gone two steps when a woman came barreling toward him, a look of fury on her narrow, overly made-up face. "I wonder who that is," I murmured to Bess and George. "She doesn't look happy."

"Hibbard!" the woman barked, stabbing a red-tipped finger toward Donald's face. "Are you a complete imbecile? A total moron? Do you even *have* a brain stem?"

"What's the matter, Madge?" Donald asked mildly, not seeming the slightest bit disturbed by her insults or the stabbing finger.

The woman waved the Styrofoam cup she was holding in her other hand. Brown liquid sloshed over the side. "This coffee is ice cold!" she shouted. "I can't drink it like this. You might as well serve me a cup of fresh mud!"

"Sorry about that, Madge." Donald reached out and expertly plucked the cup out of her hand without spilling another drop. "I'll get you a fresh cup right away."

"Good. And be quick about it," Madge spat out. Then she spun on her heel and stormed off.

"Nice lady," George said sarcastically when she was out of earshot.

"That's Madge Michaels, the assistant director," Donald explained. "She's, er, a little high-strung. Excuse me—I'd better go find her some hot coffee before she bursts a blood vessel." Giving us one last wry smile, he hurried off.

"Poor guy," Bess commented. "I know some people will do anything to be a part of Hollywood, but I sure wouldn't want to have his job."

"Whew! You're not kidding," Deb exclaimed. "I guess show business isn't all it's cracked up to be! I just hope poor Sydney knows what she's getting into by marrying a TV star."

Personally I thought the term "TV star" might be a bit too strong a description of a reality-TV contestant, but I decided to keep that opinion to myself. "Well, as a model she's used to being in the spotlight," I said instead.

"That reminds me," Deb said. "I'd better go check on Sydney and see how she's holding up. See you later!"

Bess, George, and I spent the next few minutes wandering around, saying hi to people we knew and watching the TV crew set up. When we came across Sydney, she was standing with her parents and Deb and a couple of others. She looked beautiful in a fashionable green wraparound dress, but her face was extra pale and her eyes kept skittering off toward the runway nearby. It was hard to tell whether she was anxious to see her fiancé or just nervous about this whole extravaganza. Probably both, I figured.

My friends and I were chatting with one of our old schoolteachers when a sharp whistle silenced the entire area. "Check it out," George said, nodding toward the temporary platform the TV people had set up near the runway. "It's our good pal Donald."

Sure enough, Donald Hibbard was standing up on the platform. He had a bullhorn in his hand.

"Thank you for your attention!" Donald shouted through the bullhorn. "And now, may I introduce our director, Mr. Hans Eberhart!"

My friends and I clapped politely along with everyone else as the director climbed up to stand beside Donald. Hans Eberhart was of average height and weight, with unruly gray hair, a close-cropped graying beard, and a fiercely intelligent look on his broad, weather-beaten face. He took the bullhorn from the PA.

"Thanks for coming, everyone," he said, his words tinged with a slight German accent. "I have received word that the plane will be landing in just a few moments. Please gather in the area marked off by the ropes to welcome our visitors, all right?"

"Wow, now I really feel glamorous," Bess joked as we all shuffled over to the roped-off area.

George was walking backward, craning her neck to keep an eye on the director. "I can't believe Hans Eberhart is really here," she said. "I'm dying to talk to him about his early work."

Soon the entire River Heights contingent was crowded behind the ropes. We didn't have long to wait before there was a mechanical whine from overhead. Moments later a small, sleek jet with the *Daredevils* logo printed on the side was touching down on the airstrip.

"Feel free to cheer!" Donald called out through the bullhorn, which Eberhart had given back to him.

We all dutifully clapped as the plane taxied to a stop nearby. George let out a few wolf whistles, which made everyone standing around us laugh.

Some airport employees pushed a rolling staircase up to the side of the plane. Once it was in place, the door swung open.

"Check it out!" George said, poking me on the shoulder. "That's Vic!"

I nodded, wondering just how pop-culture-clueless she thought I was. Anyone with a TV would have recognized Vic Valdez, with his trademark head of spiky black hair, his tall, lean figure, and his slouchy urban-punk style.

This time nobody had to tell the crowd to cheer. Everyone shouted and waved their arms, and I found myself swept along in the excitement, adding my own cheers to the rest. When I glanced over toward Sydney, I saw that she was probably the only person standing silently. Her eyes were trained on Vic, and there was a happy little smile on her lips that made my heart melt.

Vic spotted her, too. Leaning over the railing at the top of the rolling staircase, he blew her a kiss. Then he went back to waving at the crowds and the cameras.

After a moment another guy appeared in the doorway behind him. He was about Vic's age and height but was twice as broad, with shoulders as wide as the plane's doorway, and muscles upon muscles popping out of his tight white shirt. A huge grin stretched across his face beneath his blond buzzcut as he saluted the crowd.

"That's Bo Champion, Vic's best friend on the

show," George informed me. "The gossip columns in New York call him and Vic 'Vicbo' because they hang out together so much."

"Oh, right," Bess said. "I remember Syd mentioning him."

As Bo and Vic started down the steps, stopping and waving every few seconds, more people started pouring out of the plane. Each of them stopped to wave and pose at the top of the stairway as well.

"That's Pandora Peace," George said as a pretty blonde dressed in a flowing sixties-inspired dress appeared. "She was on the same season of *Daredevils* as Vic and Bo. She was Vic's showmance."

"His what?" I said. "Is that some reality-TV term?"

"His showmance," George repeated a bit impatiently. "You know—show romance. They flirted a lot and sort of became a couple by the end of the show. I heard it never went anywhere after that, and of course then he met Sydney. But it looks like they've stayed friends at least—" She cut herself off with a gasp. "Oh, and hey, check it out—there's Dragon!"

I looked up. The latest person to appear at the top of the stairs was a young man with an enormous dragon tattoo on his face. "Let me guess," I joked. "He got that name because he likes reading fantasy novels?"

George rolled her eyes. "He's on the current season of *Daredevils*," she said. "Apparently his goal in life is to be the white Bruce Lee. Syd said the producers insisted on making him part of the wedding party. Guess the ratings aren't where they'd like them to be this season."

"Ooh, look!" Bess put in. "There's Akinyi. Guess she made it back from Bermuda."

I glanced up curiously. Akinyi was even taller and thinner in person than she'd looked in her photo on Sydney's PDA. She cut a striking figure in a skin-tight electric-blue catsuit that set off her gleaming dark skin and hair. Like everyone else, she paused and waved gracefully at the top of the stairs, turning slightly from one side to another to allow the cameras to capture her from every angle.

"And let me guess—that must be Candy Kaine," I said as another tall, slender young woman appeared behind Akinyi. It was no wonder she and Sydney had been cast to play sisters. Their pale complexions and vibrant red hair matched perfectly, though Candy's hair was cut into a stylish shoulder-length bob.

"Excellent deduction, detective," Bess joked.

More people came out, but none of us recognized them, so we returned our attention to Vic. He was now within half a dozen steps of ground level, having stopped on almost every step for more posing and waving. The camera operators were filming the whole thing from every possible angle, with Hans Eberhart hurrying around to take the occasional peek through one of the lenses.

Then I saw the director hurrying toward the onlookers. "Come, Miss Marvin," he called, gesturing toward Sydney. "You should be at the bottom to greet your man with a nice hug and kiss, hmm?"

"Oh." Sydney blushed, looking slightly uncomfortable. "Um, okay."

She allowed the director to hustle her over to the base of the stairway. Vic's face lit up when she approached.

"There's my beautiful bride!" he called out, hurrying down the last few steps. The crowd let out a collective "awww!" as he wrapped her in his long, skinny arms and kissed her.

"Sweet," I murmured to Bess. "But Syd looks a little embarrassed, doesn't she?"

"Wouldn't you?" Bess whispered back, rolling her eyes. "Just imagine if you had a dozen TV cameras filming your next date with Ned!"

I shuddered. "No thank you!"

"Hey," George put in. "Do you guys hear sirens?"

Now that she mentioned it, I did. They were faint at first, but rapidly came closer. Soon everyone was looking toward the sound.

"What is this?" Eberhart muttered loudly. "If we have to redub this entire scene . . ."

The sirens came even closer, drowning him out. A second later a pair of police cruisers sped around the corner of the building and skidded to a stop at the edge of the airstrip.

Chief McGinnis of the River Heights Police Department climbed out of the first car. "Stop right there, everyone!" he blustered in his usual self-important way. "We've just received a tip that someone is trying to smuggle in stolen goods on this plane!"

A TASTE OF DANGER

The next few minutes were all chaos and confusion. Several people descended on the chief to protest, and there was much shouting and waving around of hands. Sydney looked horrified and perplexed. Vic seemed to waver between being outraged and tentatively amused, wondering aloud every few minutes if he was being punked.

But I watched the whole scene unfold with concern, knowing that whatever else this was, it was definitely no joke. Chief McGinnis doesn't roll that way. He takes his job very seriously, even when he's, um, not doing it very well. Trust me, I've learned that the hard way after solving a few too many of his cases for him.

Finally, though, Hans Eberhart and Ellie Marvin seemed to convince him that this was all some kind of mistake. Still, the chief insisted on sending a couple of his men up into the plane to check things out. They emerged minutes later, having found nothing suspicious, and soon the cruisers were on their way out.

"See? No biggie, dude." Bo Champion laughed loudly and clapped Vic on the back. "They're just not used to our brand of trouble out here in the sticks, yo!"

Vic seemed to settle on being amused rather than annoyed. "Okay, you're right, bro," he said. "But nobody better mess up this wedding for my gorgeous bride, or they'll have to deal with me! Where are you, sweetie?"

He glanced around for Sydney, who came hurrying toward him. I bit my lip, noting the anxious look on her face. I guessed that so far, her dream wedding wasn't unfolding quite how she'd imagined it.

"All right, everyone. That is enough of that, I think." Hans Eberhart clapped his hands, his voice carrying over the hubbub even without the bullhorn. "Now we shall move on to the party, all right? Please follow Donald."

Once again we found ourselves shuffled along like cattle. This time we ended up in a cavernous hangar at the edge of the airport's grounds. Inside, a wooden dance floor and several enormous rugs had been laid over the concrete floor. The metal walls were draped with swaths of shimmery metallic fabric, and the high ceiling was festooned with what seemed like thousands of blinking, twinkling lights. Several dozen people were already inside, including a DJ pumping out dance music, a few uniformed cater waiters, and more guests.

"Ew," George said, glaring across the room. "Looks like Deirdre squirmed her way in again."

Glancing over, I saw that she was right. Deirdre was wriggling and shimmying in front of one of the cameramen who had just come in. I also recognized more friends and acquaintances from around town. "Looks like they invited all the wedding guests," I surmised. "They must have wanted more people to fill up this huge place."

Bess was staring around the hangar. "What are they trying to do, turn this place into a hot, happening nightclub or something?"

"A hot, happening nightclub in River Heights?" I couldn't help being amused at the thought. "Yeah, it would really take the magic of television to make that happen!" I wrinkled my nose. "Too bad they couldn't do anything about the smell of jet fuel. It reeks in here."

"They probably figured it would be easy to film a party scene in this kind of space," George said, pointing to several large cameras already filming the proceedings, including a couple on tracks overhead.

"But why have a party scene at all?" Bess asked.

Before any of us could come up with an answer, Sydney hurried toward us. She was arm in arm with Vic.

"Hi, guys," she greeted us breathlessly. "I wanted you to meet Vic. Vic, these are my cousins Bess and George, and that's Nancy."

Vic grinned at us. He was surprisingly good-looking up close once you got past the wild spiky hair and weird clothes. "Yo," he said. "Nice to meet you. Syd's told me a lot about you guys."

"Ditto," George said. "I'm a big fan. But that won't stop me from tracking you down and making you sorry if you ever hurt my cousin, dude."

Sydney and I laughed, while Bess looked horrified. Vic just grinned and saluted. "I hear you, cousin," he said. "And you don't have to worry. I'd gnaw my own arm off before I'd ever hurt my beautiful lady."

"Aw, that's sweet," Bess cooed.

George shot her a look. "Are you kidding?" she said with a smirk. "I've seen every episode of *Daredevils*. Chewing his arm off is nothing compared to what this guy has done!"

That made all of us laugh. "Touché," Vic said, his grin wider than ever. "I guess that means you'll just have to trust me when I say I'd do anything to make Sydney happy."

"Vic!" someone shouted from nearby. "Hans wants you for some close-ups."

"Coming!" Vic called back. Throwing his arm around Sydney, he leaned over and planted a kiss on top of her head. "Be back soon, love," he said, then disappeared into the crowd.

Sydney gazed after him with a sigh. "Isn't he great?" she said. "Having him here makes this whole crazy wedding-planning thing a little less . . ."

"Crazy?" Bess supplied helpfully.

Sydney shrugged. "I was going to say aggravating," she said. "But crazy works too!"

Soon one of the TV people dragged Sydney off too, leaving the three of us to fend for ourselves. "Now what?" George said.

"I was thinking I'd call Tonya," I said, referring to the switchboard operator at the local police HQ. "I want to find out what kind of tip they got about that plane. It must've sounded pretty serious if it sent Chief McGinnis running out here in person."

"Don't be so sure about that," George said, swaying to the song the DJ had just put on, a fast-paced hip-hop number. "Even Chief McGinnis isn't clueless enough not to know about this whole TV-production thing."

"Of course not," Bess put in. "Syd mentioned that they had to get all kinds of permits to shoot here in town."

George ignored her. "Anyway, my guess is he was hoping to get his ugly mug on TV too. For all we know, he made up the whole story about that tip!"

I doubted that. Chief McGinnis might not be the sharpest tool in the shed, but he was pretty honest. And like I said before, he takes his job very seriously. He wasn't going to change that for a few minutes of TV fame.

Sticking my hand in my purse, I realized my cell phone wasn't in there. Drat. I belatedly remembered that I'd never put it back after charging it the previous night.

Before I could ask my friends if I could borrow one of theirs, I noticed Sydney's two model friends, Akinyi and Candy Kaine, hurrying toward us. Candy was in the lead, a big smile on her pretty face.

"Hi! Are you guys the other bridesmaids?" she asked, raising her voice to be heard over the pounding music.

"That's us," Bess replied. "Three of them, anyway. There's one more floating around here somewhere. I'm Bess, and this is George and Nancy."

"Nice to meet you. I'm Candy, and this is Akinyi."

"Hello," Akinyi said, though she seemed a little distracted. Close up, she was more impressive than ever. I tried to estimate just how tall she was—six two? Six three?

Candy elbowed her in the ribs. "Chill out, Kinnie," she said cheerfully. Then she rolled her eyes at us. "She's been worried about the lighting since we got here."

Akinyi frowned at her. "Do not mock me, girl. The lighting in here is atrocious!" she said in a voice lightly tinted with some kind of exotic accent. Now that I thought about it, I vaguely remembered Bess or maybe Sydney mentioning that Akinyi had been born somewhere in Africa before coming to the U.S. as a child. "I'll be lucky if I show up on camera at all."

"Don't pay any attention to her," Candy told us jokingly. "She's just cranky because she had to fly straight through from her shoot in Bermuda."'

"Yeah," George said. "I can see how traumatic it must be to be forced to go to Bermuda."

Akinyi shot her a strange look, not seeming to get the joke. "My skin tone doesn't work well in low light," she said. "I'll probably look terrible in this dark place!"

"You'll look fine," Candy reassured her. "I'm the

one who should be worried. I'm so pale, I'll probably look like a ghost who's haunting the party!"

We all chuckled, and even Akinyi cracked a smile. It made her look slightly less exotic but a whole lot prettier. "My friend is right," she said, sounding a bit more relaxed. "Never mind me. I'm sure Syd has already told you I'm the most neurotic person she knows."

"Not at all," Bess said. "She has only great things to say about you. Like how you helped her learn her way around New York, and how much she enjoys being your roommate . . ."

We all made polite small talk for a few minutes after that, mostly about Sydney and the wedding. Then I noticed Hans Eberhart winding his way toward us through the crowd.

"Hello, everyone," he said when he reached our little group. Bowing toward the two models, he added, "Ladies, it is wonderful to have you involved in this production. Please, enjoy the party, and do feel free to circulate." He waved his hand around the room. More people had arrived, though I didn't recognize most of them. I wondered if some of them were TV people dressed up to look like guests.

George was grinning like a fool. "Hi, Mr. Eberhart!" she said, her voice oddly high-pitched and breathy. "It's so awesome to meet you! I'm probably your biggest fan. I've seen your first film, *Fall from Grace*, like, a million times—I even had the opening scene as my computer wallpaper for a while. And of course I watch *Daredevils* every week, and . . ."

Bess and I traded an amused look as she rattled on. George generally likes to play the world-weary cynic. It was rare—and sort of entertaining—to see her go all fangirly.

She was still chattering eagerly at the director when I saw someone else approaching the group. I recognized him as one of those anonymous extra people who'd emerged from the plane behind the celebrities.

"Ah, there you are, darling," Akinyi greeted the newcomer fondly, leaning down to kiss him on the forehead. She had to lean *way* down. The guy was at least six inches shorter than she was, and maybe four or five years older. He was thin and stoop-shouldered, with receding mouse-brown hair, round rimless glasses, and skin so pasty it looked as if it had never seen sunlight. Akinyi took his arm and glanced around the group. "Please let me introduce my boyfriend, Josh Kochman, everybody," she said proudly. "He's a very talented screenwriter."

Whatever I might have expected a fashion model's boyfriend to look like, Josh wasn't it. Akinyi introduced all of us, but Josh did little more than nod hello before turning all his attention toward Eberhart.

"It's an honor to meet you, sir," he said. "As Akinyi said, I'm a screenwriter, and I was really hoping to talk to you about my latest project. It's a sort of horror-humor-suspense-love story with a twist, totally retro in an art-punk kind of way. The story begins with a beautiful woman who turns to a wisecracking scientist for help after nearly being killed by a swarm of genetically altered beetles. . . ."

"Come on," Bess murmured in my ear. "I think it's time to take his advice and circulate. Otherwise I have a feeling we'll be hearing the whole screenplay."

I nodded. Dragging along the rather reluctant George, we excused ourselves and wandered off, leaving the models and Josh with the director.

"Now what?" George said.

"Now I call Tonya and see what she knows," I said. "Can I borrow a phone?"

Bess pulled hers out of her handbag. "Do you really think there's a mystery here, Nancy?" she asked. "I mean, the police tip is a little weird, and so is that RSVP. But these *Daredevils* guys do seem pretty wild—what if they really are the ones behind this?"

"Then I'm going to bust them so Syd can relax a little," I said, already dialing.

Unfortunately, the person who answered told me

that Tonya had the day off. I left a message for her to call me the next day, then returned Bess's phone.

"So much for that," I told my friends. "Come on, let's go find Sydney. I want to ask her if she and Vic have any enemies that they know of."

Finding Sydney in the airport-hangar-turned-fake-nightclub proved to be easier said than done. We swam through the crowds of people, but there was no sign of her distinctive red hair.

"There's that Donald PA guy," George said, pointing. "Maybe you should ask him where Sydney is. He seems to be in charge of keeping track of everything and everyone around here."

"Maybe later. He looks a little busy right now." I grimaced, noting that Madge, the foul-tempered assistant director, appeared to be haranguing the PA again. He nodded a few times without speaking, then hurried off and disappeared while Madge stalked off in the direction of one of the camera operators.

My friends and I wandered toward the temporary dance floor, where Pandora Peace was doing some kind of elaborate interpretive dance in her bare feet, not seeming to notice or mind that she was out there all alone. She wasn't lonely for long, though—as we watched, Bo Champion and Dragon ran out and starting dancing with her. Bo and Pandora were soon laughing and goofing off, each of them throwing in more and more outrageous dance moves to try to one-up each other. Meanwhile Dragon stayed a little apart, dancing athletically while his eyes shot around toward the nearest cameras.

At that moment I finally spotted Sydney. She was standing off to one side with Deb, now joined by Candy, watching the action on the dance floor.

"There's Syd," I told my friends. "Let's go talk to her."

We made our way toward the trio. Before we got there, I heard a commotion from the dance floor. Glancing that way, I saw Vic being pushed out onto the floor by Madge, the ill-tempered assistant director. He was laughing and protesting loudly that he didn't feel like dancing. But Bo waved to him.

"Get out here, bro!" he called. "Show the people how it's done!"

"Oh, all right!" Vic exclaimed as Madge backed off. "If you insist . . ."

With that, he broke into a series of gravity-defying dance moves, jumping and spinning around to the beat. Bo and Dragon joined in, while Pandora clapped along nearby. The activity was attracting lots of attention all through the party, and people crowded closer for a better look, blocking Sydney from my view.

The song ended and everyone applauded. "And now for something a little slower," the DJ crooned into his mic as a slow ballad poured out of the speakers. "Miss Pandora Peace requests this dance from Mr. Valdez—for old times' sake."

"What? I did not!" Pandora exclaimed, laughing.

Meanwhile Vic was glancing off the floor, searching the crowd. "Where's my girl?" he said, squinting against the bright colored lights pulsing toward him from the edge of the dance floor. "This dance should be for her."

Madge reappeared, this time pushing Vic toward Pandora. "Go on, you two," she urged. "Just one friendly little dance. For the fans."

I shook my head, guessing what was going on. The TV people wanted to give their viewers what they wanted, which was a reunion of the Vic-Pandora "showmance." And they didn't seem to care how Vic—or Sydney—might feel about that.

"So much for reality," I muttered.

"Huh?" Bess said, watching as Vic finally held out one hand gallantly toward Pandora, laughing sheepishly. Pandora gave a cute little curtsy and took his hand, and the two of them began playfully slow-dancing.

"Come on." I turned away. "Sydney could probably use some distraction right about now. Let's see if we can talk to her."

It took only a moment to reach Sydney, who was

still standing with Candy and Deb. It took even less time than that to see that she wasn't happy about what was going on out on the dance floor.

"Never mind," Deb was saying cheerily. "You're the one he's marrying, right?"

That didn't seem to give Sydney much comfort. "I knew this filming was a mistake," she said. "When the cameras are on, Vic just forgets everything else." She sniffed. "Including me, I guess."

I winced. Sydney could be a little high-strung at the best of times, but this was beyond that. She looked really upset.

I was about to suggest we step outside or something, just so she could get away from the sight of her fiancé slow-dancing with Pandora. But Candy beat me to it, putting a protective arm around Sydney's slim shoulders.

"I could use some fresh air," she said. "Come on, let's go outside for a bit, okay?"

Sydney sniffed again, merely shrugging in response. But she went along as Candy steered her firmly toward the nearest exit. Deb stared after them, shifting her weight from one foot to the other as if uncertain whether to follow.

It was tempting to follow them myself. But I figured Sydney wasn't in the mood for my interrogation just then, so instead I turned to see what was happening out on the dance floor.

I was just in time to see a couple of Mrs. Fayne's waiters wheeling out a cart with a huge crystal bowl on it. "What's going on?" Bess asked.

George squinted toward the bowl, which was filled with vibrant purple liquid. "Oh, I remember Mom talking about this," she said. "The producers requested it—it's a punch bowl filled with PowerUp."

"You mean the sports drink?" I asked.

George nodded. "It's one of the main sponsors of the show. Mom had to buy up every case of the stuff in River Heights to make sure she had enough to fill up that stupid punch bowl. She sent a couple of people over early with it—figured they'd have to spend, like, an hour opening and pouring to make sure it was ready for the big moment."

The song ended and the DJ came on again, reciting what sounded like a mini-commercial for PowerUp before inviting everyone out onto the floor for a drink of the stuff. "We'll start with the happy groom and his buddies from the world's most powered-up show, *Daredevils*!" he finished.

Vic, Bo, Pandora, and Dragon all whooped and pumped their fists. Then Vic hurried over to grab the first cup of PowerUp from the catering employee who was scooping it out.

"Hang on, Vic," the DJ said. "I know it looks

delicious, but don't drink it yet, buddy. We want to let your wedding party give a toast to your happy day. So let's get everyone powered up first."

Madge joined the employee, busily passing out cups to Pandora, Bo, and Dragon. Akinyi had just wandered over, but when Madge tried to shove a cup into her hand, she waved her off.

"None for me, thanks," she said. "Too many calories."

"Anyone else?" Madge called out, holding up the cup. "We want the whole wedding party up here for the toast!"

"Let's not and say we did," George muttered to Bess and me. "I've had grape PowerUp before. I tried it when they first started advertising it on *Daredevils*, actually. Trust me, the stuff is vile. Even my brothers wouldn't touch it after the first sip, and they'll eat or drink just about anything."

Meanwhile Deb pushed her way to the front of the crowd, giggling. "I'm in the wedding party," she said. "But no PowerUp for me. I'm allergic to caffeine."

Madge just shrugged and set the cup back on the table. "Where's Hans?" she said, glancing around.

She spotted the director at the same time I did. He was standing a short distance away with Josh. It looked as if the would-be screenwriter was still bending his ear about his ideas.

Madge shrugged and clapped her hands. "Let's proceed, people!" she called out. "Vic—a toast, if you please?" Then she backed off out of camera range.

Vic cleared his throat and stepped to the center of the floor, holding his cup aloft. "First of all, where's my blushing bride?" he called out. "She should be up here with me!"

"She went outside for a while," George called.

Vic looked disappointed, lowering his cup. "Should we wait for her?" he called to the assistant director.

"Just go!" Madge called back. "We can stick her in during postproduction."

Yeah. So much for reality, I thought again.

Vic shrugged and lifted the cup back up. "Okay, whatever," he said with a laugh. "Thanks for coming, everyone. It's cool to be here with my best girl and my best friends. Bottoms up!"

He lifted the cup to his lips while everyone else was echoing the "bottoms up." But he'd barely tipped it for the first sip when his eyes widened, and he tossed the cup away, spitting all over the floor.

"Stop! Don't drink it!" he shouted at the top of his lungs. "There's, like, gasoline or something in it!"

IN SICKNESS AND IN HEALTH

I couldn't believe the film crew was still filming at the hospital. Most of us were sort of milling around the reception area, much to the confusion of the nurses and receptionists on duty. Vic had been whisked off to a room right away, accompanied by Sydney and her parents. But since nobody else had even come close to drinking the jet fuel–laced PowerUp, the staff didn't seem to know what to do with us.

"It's a good thing Vic's used to eating and drinking all kinds of weird stuff on the show," George commented. She was flopped on one of the couches in the waiting area, flipping through a dusty old magazine she'd grabbed from the end table. "It might have taken a normal person longer to recognize the smell and taste of jet fuel."

"Ya think?" Bess said sarcastically, leaning against the back of the couch. "I mean, I certainly don't go around drinking jet fuel every day of the week myself."

"It's also lucky that nobody thought Vic was kidding around and drank the stuff anyway," I said with a shudder. "Anyway, one thing's for sure. There's definitely a mystery here."

The police had already come and gone. One of the officers who'd responded was a friend of mine, and he'd confirmed Vic's suspicions. The sports drink appeared to have been laced with a small amount of jet fuel.

"True," George agreed. "As nuts as the *Daredevils* guys might be, I doubt they'd actually try to poison one another. Besides, they pretty much stick to just messing around within their own little group as far as I know. I can't see them trying to involve innocent bystanders."

"So then who did it?" I mused aloud. "And how, and why?"

"How? Well, it's no mystery where someone got the jet fuel," Bess said. "I mean, we were at the airport, right?"

"Right," I said, glancing around the room. "And that means it was probably someone at the party who did it."

"Had to be," George agreed. "You saw the security at the airport. And we know it wasn't my mom or her people, so someone must've added the jet fuel after the PowerUp got to the party."

As the caterers of the event, Mrs. Fayne and her crew had been first in line for suspicion—at least as far as the police were concerned. But I hadn't bothered with that possibility for a second. All the employees working the party had been with her for a while. And of course I knew Mrs. Fayne herself had nothing to do with it.

I decided that as long as we were all stuck at the hospital together, we might as well start poking around a little. Parting ways, we all headed off to talk to people and find out whatever we could. I decided to start with a college kid named Terrence who was one of the cater waiters. He was crouched on the edge of a chair looking anxious.

"Hey," I said, perching on the next chair. "You okay?"

"I hope so, Nancy," Terrence replied miserably. "If I lose this job, I'll never be able to pay my car insurance!"

"You won't lose your job," I assured him. "Whatever happened today, it wasn't your fault."

"But Andrea and I were the ones who got that punch bowl ready," he exclaimed. "We spent all morning pouring that stupid purple stuff into it."

"Did the punch bowl smell funny or anything?"

"No way. It was all dusty from being in storage in Mrs. F's basement, so Andrea spent, like, twenty minutes scrubbing it out." Terrence shook his head. "Trust me, it was clean when we started filling it. And before you can ask, yes, all the bottles of PowerUp were sealed. No funny smells there, either."

"Where was the punch bowl between when you filled it and when you guys brought it out for the toast?" I asked.

"In the foyer off this little office-type room at the back of the hangar," he replied. "We did most of the setup in the bigger part of the room, but we stuck the punch out there so nobody would bump into it and spill it."

"A foyer? So was there a door to the outside?"

Terrence nodded. "Actually there were doors in both rooms," he said. "Our staff and some of those TV people were going in and out all day. Andrea joked that maybe the TV peeps missed New York, because it was like Grand Central Station back there."

Thanking him for the information, I left him to his worries. I thought about going over to talk to

Andrea next. She'd been with Mrs. Fayne just as long as Terrence and was just as unlikely a suspect in my opinion. But there was always a chance she'd noticed something he hadn't.

Just then there was a burst of raucous laughter. Glancing that way, I saw that Bo, Pandora, and Dragon were hanging out together at the far end of the room. A cameraman was filming their every move.

That reminded me that the entire party had been caught on film. I wondered if the police had asked for access to the footage to see if anyone had left the party at a suspicious time.

I wish I could get a look at those tapes myself, I thought, glancing from one camera to the next. *Then again, maybe there wouldn't be much point. That hangar has a bunch of doors, and anyone could've come or gone for perfectly innocent reasons. Besides, I seriously doubt the cameras ever went back into the catering prep areas. . . .*

Another burst of laughter broke into my thoughts. The Daredevils seemed pretty cheerful after their near-death experience. Then again, I supposed that was sort of the point of the show.

Wandering over, I smiled at them. "Hey," I said. "I'm Nancy, one of the bridesmaids. So I hear Vic is going to be okay."

Bo turned serious immediately. "He better be," he blustered, clenching his meaty fists. "If anyone hurts my bro like that, or messes up his big day with his lady . . ."

Pandora gave him a shove. "Chill out, man," she said. "Vic's fine. I knew he would be. He's got karma on his side."

Dragon didn't say anything. He just stared at me as if trying to figure out who I was and why I was talking to them.

Just then the cameraman shifted positions, still filming away. I glanced at him, feeling a bit self-conscious.

At the same time, Dragon cleared his throat and sat up a little straighter. I guess he'd just remembered the camera was there too, because it was like he suddenly came to life and went into full performance mode.

"Dude," he announced to no one in particular, "it's a good thing I wasn't the one who tasted that first sip instead of Vic." He pounded his chest with one fist. "See, I've got a cast-iron stomach. I can handle anything!"

Pandora rolled her eyes. "You mean like *death*?" she said with more sarcasm than I might have expected from a hippie chick. "You can handle that, huh? Wow, you must be even more talented than you're always telling us."

Bo snorted with laughter. I cleared my throat, still doing my best to ignore the camera. "So listen," I said. "Who do you guys think did it? Um, does Vic have any enemies or anything?"

All three of them turned to stare at me. "Who are you again?" Bo asked.

"Nancy," I said. "Bridesmaid."

Dragon shrugged. "Every celebrity has enemies," he said, flicking a speck of dust off his bicep. "Nature of the beast."

Just then Akinyi and Candy hurried over. "This is out of control!" Akinyi blurted out immediately. "How can everyone just sit around talking and acting like this isn't happening? I can't stand it!"

"Easy, Kinnie." Candy looked distraught too, though she seemed to be holding it together a little better than the other model. "Vic's going to be okay, remember? Freaking out isn't going to help anyone, including yourself."

Akinyi shuddered and waved her slim hands as if pushing away her friend's words. "You didn't see it, Candy!" she cried. "You were outside. It was horrible! Horrible!"

Pandora got up and hurried over to Akinyi, looking concerned. "Please, darling," she said soothingly, rubbing Akinyi's back. "Don't do this to yourself. Gather your spiritual energy and resist the negative forces. I can already see that your aura is in crisis. . . ."

Bo and Dragon were just staring at Akinyi, not

seeming to know what to say as she melted down in front of them. I knew how they felt. I remembered Akinyi joking around about being neurotic earlier; maybe that wasn't such a joke after all.

I turned to Candy. "That's right, I almost forgot you and Syd went outside before it happened," I said. "Did you see or hear anything weird while you were out there?"

Candy bit her lip and shook her head. "No, and I'm really glad we didn't. Syd's pretty shaken up about this. I can't even imagine how she'd be taking it if she'd witnessed it all."

Pandora nodded. "The poor thing. I hope she can recover her joyous spirit of love after this. Maybe I can help by doing a reading for her—does anyone know where I can get some tea leaves?"

Deciding I wasn't likely to learn much more from anyone in that group at the moment, I quietly extricated myself and wandered off. Spotting Bess and George, I hurried over to rejoin them.

"Hi," I greeted them, quickly filling them in on the little I'd learned. "You guys find out anything interesting?"

"Not really. George and I got stuck for most of the time talking to Syd's friend Deb," Bess said. "She's all aflutter."

Despite the serious situation, I smiled. Only Bess

could get away with using a word like "aflutter." But I had to admit it suited Deb's usual demeanor perfectly.

"Yeah," George put in. "She kept babbling about how she couldn't believe something like this could happen right here in good ol' River Heights."

"If she only knew!" I joked, thinking back over the countless criminals, wrongdoers, and assorted bad guys I'd busted over the years right there in our sleepy little Midwestern city. "Anyway, from talking to Terrence I think it's safe to speculate that the punch probably got poisoned while it was waiting off in that little side room."

George shrugged. "Okay, but what does that tell us?" she said. "Anyone at the party could've sneaked in there, either through the catering prep room or by going outside and then back in the other door."

"Yeah, I know. Doesn't help us much." I shot a look at the closest camera, which was being wielded by a burly man with bushy eyebrows, a gleaming bald head, and a grumpy expression. "Although if we could check out the footage and see who might've left at an opportune time . . ."

My voice trailed off as I heard a commotion from nearby. We were standing at the edge of the waiting area, very close to the arched doorway leading out to the hospital's main entrance. Stepping closer, I peered out and saw Deirdre there talking to someone with a camera.

However, that someone wasn't part of the *Daredevils* crew. The familiar logo of one of the local news teams was plastered all over the camera.

". . . and it was just such a near-tragedy," Deirdre exclaimed, a single tear wending its way down her cheek. "Just imagine if everyone at the party had taken a drink of that stuff—the carnage! The horror! What kind of terrible person would do something like that to a bunch of innocent people?"

Uh-oh. One glance at the reporter holding the microphone up to Deirdre's face told me that he was eating this up. If the local press ran with the over-dramatized story Deirdre was spouting, the *Daredevils* TV crew would be the least of Sydney's problems. More important, the culprit might get nervous enough to back off. That would make it much harder to figure out who'd done it.

"What is it?" Bess asked as I ducked back into the waiting room and glanced around.

"Deirdre," I said succinctly. "She's spilling her guts to the TV news out there."

"Want me to go out and tell her off?" George offered eagerly, already taking a step toward the entry-way. "I can explain to the reporters that Deirdre's brain is only the size of a pea and so they shouldn't listen to a word she says."

Bess grabbed her by the arm to stop her as I shook my head. "Thanks, but I think we'd better let the TV people take care of it," I said. "They're the experts at handling this sort of thing, I'd imagine."

"True," George agreed reluctantly. "*Daredevils* is always having to deal with the local press while they're filming. Like the time the contestants got busted by the local decency police for swimming across the Mississippi River naked in January . . ."

I left Bess alone to hear the rest of the anecdote. I'd just spotted Hans Eberhart wandering across the room nearby chatting with one of the camera operators. Hurrying over, I politely interrupted their conversation and asked to speak privately with the director. Once the cameraman had hurried off to film Sydney's father, who had just wandered out into the waiting room, I explained to Eberhart what was happening just outside.

The director listened, stroking his stubbly beard. Then he thanked me and called over Madge, the assistant director. "We have a press situation out in the lobby," he told her calmly. "Please handle it."

Madge nodded shortly. "I'm on it."

She took off across the waiting room, her high heels clicking on the tile floor. I winced, recalling the way she'd yelled at Donald the PA. Maybe this time Deirdre would meet her match!

"Good," Hans said. "That should take care of it. Madge, she is a piranha—it's why I put up with her other, er, idiosyncrasies." He chuckled with amusement.

I smiled along. "Yes, she should be able to take care of that problem easily enough," I said. "But, um, have you thought about maybe backing off on this filming for a little while, sir? You know—just until the police get a handle on who might have done this."

Eberhart stared at me with what appeared to be genuine astonishment. "Stop filming?" he said. "You mean now, just when this is turning from a bit of vanity fluff into something much more interesting?"

"But that's my point," I said. "Someone appears to be seeking attention by trying to sabotage things. Why give that person what he or she wants?"

Eberhart shook his head. "No, no, my dear, you don't understand," he said patiently, as if explaining things to a dull-witted child. "This danger, this sabotage, it is quite within the spirit of what *Daredevils* is all about. The audience, they will eat it up with a spoon." He finished by mimicking lifting a spoon to his mouth, complete with an enthusiastic smacking of lips.

"I understand, sir," I said. "But this isn't just a TV

show. It's real life. If whoever's doing this escalates the sabotage and someone gets really hurt—"

"Hans! There you are!" I was interrupted by Josh, Akinyi's nerdy-looking boyfriend. He rushed up to us, barely seeming to notice my presence as he zeroed in on the director. "Listen, what happened today made me rethink the revenge scene in my screenplay. What do you think if instead of the heroine tossing the beetles into the wood chipper, she tricks them into ingesting pollen laced with bug spray, or . . ."

There was more, but I didn't bother trying to keep up with his torrent of words. Eberhart, on the other hand, was nodding along with interest. Realizing I'd been dismissed, I wandered back to my friends, feeling troubled.

"Did they take care of Deirdre?" Bess asked.

"Hmm? Oh, her. Yeah, Eberhart sent Madge out to do it. But listen—do you think he could possibly have anything to do with what's been happening?"

"You mean Hans Eberhart? Are you kidding?" George looked scandalized. "He's not some two-bit hack who needs to drum up scandal to get work. He's an artist! A much better one than people give him credit for."

"Right," I said. "You keep saying he's so talented that he should have a better career. What if he agrees—and is trying to get himself noticed this way?"

Bess's eyes widened. "You mean he's setting up the sabotage so the show—and he—will get more attention?"

"Maybe. I have to admit, it sounds like a wild theory," I admitted. "But he certainly had the access. Nobody would think twice about him rushing in and out of any doors in the place earlier. And he'd probably have no trouble getting his hands on one of Syd's invitations, so he could have set up that mock one, and sent the e-mails. . . ."

I let my voice trail off, thinking over what I was saying. It really did sound a little nuts. Then again, it wasn't any crazier than anything some culprits in my past cases had done.

"I don't know, Nancy," Bess said dubiously. "Do you really think—"

She never got the chance to finish her question. Deb Camden came rushing up to us, wringing her hands.

"Oh my gosh, you guys!" she cried, her eyes wide and horrified. "You've got to come help me talk some sense into Sydney. She's so freaked out by what happened to Vic that she's threatening to call off the wedding!"

CLUES AND ALIBIS

Deb was pointing down the hall leading to the patient rooms, which was a few yards from where we were standing. I turned that way just in time to see Sydney burst out from the hallway with her mother and Vic right behind her.

"No!" Sydney wailed, her face streaked with tears and her pale cheeks red and splotchy. "I can't handle it. It's too much!"

"Sydney, settle down!" Ellie said firmly. She glanced around the waiting room, obviously realizing that just about everyone had stopped their own conversations to turn and stare.

"Hang on, Mama Ellie. Let me try, okay?" Vic put

an arm around Sydney's shoulders. "Come with me, baby," he said, his voice softer and more emotional than I'd heard it so far. "Let's just go talk about this, okay? Please, Syd?"

Sydney sniffled but didn't protest as he steered her back down the hallway out of sight—and hearing—of the waiting room. The rest of us watched them go.

"Whoa," Bess said quietly. "Sydney seems really upset."

I shot a glance at Deb, who had wandered off to talk excitedly at Candy and Akinyi. "Yeah," I agreed quietly. "It seems pretty extreme." I gestured to my friends. "Come here, we need to talk about this."

Soon we were huddled in a corner of the room well out of earshot of the rest of the people in the waiting room—and out of view of any of the TV cameras. "What's up?" George asked. "Did you have one of your hunches or something? Sleuth-O-Meter going off?"

"Not exactly." I took a deep breath, feeling a bit guilty for what I was about to say. "But listen—do either of you think it's weird that Syd would threaten to call off the wedding because of this?"

"Not really," Bess said with a shrug. "I mean, her fiancé could've been killed. That would be enough to shake up almost anyone."

George nodded. "And we all know Syd can be a little high-strung."

"I know, I know." I shook my head. "I guess that's sort of my point. What if she has cold feet, or maybe just wants out of this TV deal, and is sabotaging her own wedding?"

My friends stared at me. "No way," George said. "Syd wouldn't do that."

"She's right," Bess added. "Besides, she couldn't have spiked that PowerUp. I'm pretty sure she was front and center the whole time we were at the airport—someone would've noticed and said something if she'd disappeared off by herself, even for a few seconds."

George nodded, leaning back against the wall. "And when she *did* go outside right before it happened, Candy was with her, remember?"

"True." I'd already thought of that myself. "But she could have an accomplice or something."

Bess waved her hands. "What are we doing, sitting around here discussing this like it could actually be true?" she exclaimed. "I mean, come on! Even if Syd did want to get out of this wedding, she'd never do something so horrible. Vic could have died if he'd swallowed that jet fuel!"

"You're right, you're right. It was just a theory." I sighed. "So where does that leave us?"

"Well, there's that director guy," Bess said uncertainly. "Do you still think he's a suspect?"

"A pretty weak one at best," I admitted, my gaze roving around the waiting room. "The trouble is, no better suspects are leaping out at me based on what we saw today."

There was a burst of sudden laughter from across the room. Glancing that way, George wrinkled her nose. "What about Pandora?" she said. "Everyone knows she and Vic were an item during their season of the show. What if she's still in love with him?"

"It's possible, I guess." I looked over at Pandora, who was once again goofing around with her two fellow Daredevils. "Then again, if we're speculating about motives, we could also say that Bo or Dragon could be envious of Vic's huge popularity on the show and trying to get back at him."

"Basically, we don't know most of the people involved well enough to start guessing at stuff like that," Bess pointed out. "Shouldn't we stick to the facts and go from there?"

I smiled. "You're right, detective," I said. "So let's talk about the facts. Who could have slipped away long enough to poison the PowerUp?"

"I don't know, but I just remembered something else," George said, straightening up. "Some people weren't exactly jumping forward to join in the PowerUp toast."

Bess glanced at her. "Yeah. Like us."

"No, that's different," George said. "Nobody cared if we got up there for the photo op—we're nobodies. But people were trying to get all the celebs to join in, remember?"

My eyes widened as I realized she was right. "All the Daredevils stepped up," I said. "And a few others, too."

"But not Akinyi," Bess finished. "But are you sure that means anything? She said she didn't want the extra calories. That certainly seems like a valid reason coming from a professional fashion model."

George glanced across the room at the statuesque model, who was talking with Candy and Deb and a couple of other people while the burly bald cameraman with the bushy eyebrows filmed their every move. "Yeah," she said. "But Akinyi definitely looks like the type who comes by her skinny naturally. I can't imagine she couldn't spare a few calories in honor of her best friend's wedding."

Bess still looked doubtful. "I just can't believe one of Syd's best friends would do this. It's not like Akinyi was the only one who refused the PowerUp—Deb didn't want to drink it either, remember? And you guys aren't jumping all over her about it."

"Maybe we should." I glanced at Deb, who appeared keyed up by the latest excitement as she chattered at the others. "I just don't think we can write off anybody as a potential suspect until we figure out what's going on."

"Except for Sydney," Bess said. "Like I was saying before. And I guess that lets out Candy, too, since she was with her when it happened."

At that moment I spotted Sydney and Vic emerging once again from the back hallway. His arm was still around her, and he was murmuring quietly into her ear. She'd cleaned up her face, and while her cheeks were still pink with emotion, her expression seemed calmer than it had a few minutes earlier.

"They're back," Bess said, spotting the couple at the same time. "Looks like Vic talked her down."

"Good," I said, observing them. For once, Vic wasn't sparing even a brief glance at the cameras, which had zeroed in on the pair as soon as they'd appeared. All his attention was focused on his bride-to-be. Actually, judging by the way he was gazing at her with sweet concern in his eyes, I wasn't sure he remembered the cameras were there at all—or any of the rest of us, either. For the first time, I started to see a hint of what Sydney might see in him.

Sydney's mother bustled past them and clapped her hands for attention. "All right, everyone," she called out. "The doctors have released us, so you all might as well clear out. I think it's safe to say the welcome party is over."

◆ ◆ ◆

I called Sydney the next morning, hoping to talk over the case with her. But she sounded rushed and distracted as soon as she picked up the phone.

"Sorry, I can't talk now," she said apologetically. "I'm on my way out to get my hair and makeup done. We're doing that filming at the stadium today, remember?"

As soon as she said it, I vaguely recalled what she meant. Along with the normal wedding preparations, Sydney was expected to participate in several extra TV shoots. Today, Friday morning, she and her model friends were supposed to get together with the *Daredevils* gang to act out some unusual international wedding traditions for the cameras. It all sounded pretty silly to me. Fortunately, as noncelebrity members of the wedding party, my friends and I weren't expected—or even invited, for that matter—to join in.

"Oh, right," I said, disappointed that our chat would have to wait. After all, the wedding was a week from tomorrow, which didn't leave much time to get to the bottom of things. "Well, maybe later, then. Have fun!"

"I'll try." Sydney didn't sound too optimistic.

After I hung up, I just stood there in the hallway of my house for a moment, staring at my phone and wondering how to proceed. I was still deep in thought when Hannah Gruen came downstairs. Hannah has been our housekeeper ever since my mom died when I was three. She's definitely a member of the family as far as Dad and I are concerned.

"What are you up to today, Nancy?" she asked. "Feel like some shopping? I need to pick up a few things at the mall."

"Sorry, Hannah, I can't," I said, snapping out of my thoughts. "I think I need to be somewhere else this morning."

An hour later, I was walking across the parking lot of the River Heights University Stadium, Bess and George at my side.

"Are you sure they're going to let us in?" Bess asked as we neared the main gate. "Security has been pretty tight around this whole production."

"Probably be even tighter after what happened yesterday," George agreed. "Haven't you ever heard of a closed set, Nance? We're not on the list for today's shoot."

"We'll get in," I said with more confidence than I felt. "How can they turn us away? We're Sydney's bridesmaids."

Unfortunately, the large man standing guard at the entrance didn't seem particularly impressed when I shared that with him. "Sorry," he said, scanning a sheet of paper on the clipboard he was holding. "Not on the list."

I bit my lip, frustrated. I'd decided we didn't have any time to waste if I wanted to solve this mystery before the wedding. Besides, if the saboteur struck again during today's filming, I wanted to be there.

"But we just need to talk to Sydney," I insisted. "If you call her and tell her we're here—"

Before I could finish, I spotted Candy and Akinyi coming toward us from inside the stadium. Both of them were dressed in Hawaiian-style outfits, complete with grass skirts.

"Hi!" Candy greeted us, sounding a little distracted. "What are you guys doing here? I thought you weren't stuck doing these silly little wedding skits like we are."

"We're not," I said. "We just wanted to come watch—you know, help out if we're needed."

Meanwhile Akinyi was peering out through the gate. "You haven't seen Sydney, have you?" she asked us anxiously. "She's late, and Hans is not happy."

"We haven't seen her," I said. "But I talked to her on the phone a little earlier, and she was running a few minutes late. I'm sure she'll be here soon."

"Told you so," Candy said to Akinyi. "Honestly, do you really have to turn everything into a huge drama fest?"

Her tone was one of fond exasperation, but Akinyi

replied seriously. "Can you blame me, after all that has happened?" she said. "But never mind. Let's go back in." She glanced at the guard. "Oh, and it's okay," she added, her grass skirt rustling as she waved a hand at me and my friends. "You can let them in."

"Right," Candy added. "They're with us."

The guard shot me a skeptical glance, then shrugged. "If you say so," he muttered, waving us by.

"Thanks," I told the models as all five of us hurried through the tunnel leading into the stadium. "That guy was taking his job pretty seriously."

George chuckled. "Yeah. I don't think we were going to get past him if you two hadn't turned up when you did."

"No problem," Akinyi replied with a smile.

There was no answer from Candy. Glancing over, I saw that her attention was focused on something out on the field. Or, rather, some*one*. When I followed her gaze, it led directly to Vic. He was standing on the stadium's artificial turf, flexing his muscles as a couple of cameras filmed him. Like the models, he was dressed in a grass skirt and little else.

Akinyi noticed too. "You always did spot him first off, didn't you?" she said with a slight smile. "Too bad he only had eyes for your sister."

Candy shot her a sour look. "Very funny," she muttered. "Come on, let's get down there."

My friends and I followed the pair down the nearest set of steps leading onto the field, which was a hive of activity. People were rushing around everywhere I looked, and weird props and bits of scenery were scattered all over the field. Someone had erected a fake pyramid near the fifty-yard line, near which several horses grazed contentedly on a large pile of hay or sipped from a large water trough. At the base of the steps we were descending at the moment, someone had created what appeared to be a small tropical beach, complete with sand, shells, and a full-size palm tree.

Even as I took in the unusual scene, I couldn't help wondering what that weird little exchange between the two models had been about. But before I could ponder it much, we all heard a familiar voice behind us breathlessly calling out, "I'm here, I'm here!"

It was Sydney. She rushed into the stadium with her mother behind her. Sydney looked beautiful— she was dressed in what I assumed was supposed to be a Hawaiian-style wedding gown. It was pure white, but the fabric included a white-on-white Hawaiian print. Sydney's red hair was swept up into a loose updo, only a few tendrils spilling out over her bare shoulders.

Most of the camera crew came hurtling toward them to film the bride's arrival. I had to jump out of the way as the bushy-browed cameraman almost crashed into me.

"Excuse us! Please step aside, if you don't mind." Donald the PA came bustling up to us, smiling apologetically. "Sorry, you guys. The bride's entrance is part of the show. Can you watch from over there?"

We obediently stepped back out of camera range. Donald rushed away as Vic strode toward his bride, beaming happily. Sydney paused at the edge of the fake beach as her mother hurried off out of view. Bo and Dragon, both attired similarly to Vic, took their places next to the other two models in the background.

"Aloha, my beautiful bride!" Vic said loudly, sweeping into a bow. "I wish to welcome you with the traditions of the island of Hawaii, where the two of us decided to announce our love to the world by becoming engaged."

I might not have known Vic very well yet, but I couldn't help noticing that the words didn't exactly sound like something he would come up with on his own. Glancing over, I saw that Donald was holding up cue cards just off camera.

"So this is reality TV, huh?" Bess whispered into my ear. "Interesting version of 'reality,' isn't it?"

I grinned at her. When I turned my attention back to what was happening, I saw that Vic had just swept a lush Hawaiian lei out of a rustic-looking wooden box on the "beach" nearby. The lei was similar to the ones Akinyi and Candy were already wearing, but this one was pure white, bursting with gorgeous orchids and other tropical-looking flowers.

"Aloha nui loa," Vic said as he draped the lei over Sydney's head.

Sydney blushed. *"Aloha nui loa,"* she said shyly as the flowers settled around her neck. She smiled up at Vic, looking blissfully happy.

"What's all that aloha stuff mean?" George muttered. "I hope there are going to be subtitles with this thing."

Vic was smiling down at his bride. He leaned closer, clearly about to go in for a kiss.

But suddenly Sydney's expression changed. Her eyes widened, she let out a yelp of alarm, and her hands flew up toward the white lei.

"Ow!" she cried, yanking at the lei and dancing up and down. She let out a shriek of pain as she tugged at it. "They're biting me!" she exclaimed, doing her best to rip the lei off over her head. "They're biting me!"

I gasped. Clearly visible against Sydney's creamy skin were hundreds of tiny black insects swarming all over her neck and shoulders!

REALITY BITES

"They're ants!" Vic shouted, grabbing the lei and ripping it off Sydney's neck, sending white petals flying in every directions.

"Oh my gosh—somebody do something!" Donald the PA exclaimed, hurrying forward and flapping his hands helplessly in Sydney's direction.

Meanwhile Sydney was still crying out in pain as she spun in circles, trying frantically to brush off the tiny insects. My friends and I rushed forward to help, along with Sydney's mother, Candy and Akinyi, and most of the other people within view. But I was blocked by the bushy-browed cameraman, who stepped in front of me for a better view, filming every second of Sydney's distress.

"Excuse us!" Bess said firmly, trying to push past him.

That did about as much good as trying to shove aside the Sears Tower. The cameraman held his ground, ignoring us. "This is great stuff," he muttered with a barely muffled, rather mean-spirited guffaw. "Awesome."

We managed to dodge around him just in time to see Vic brush Donald, the other models, and Aunt Ellie aside. "I've got this," he said grimly, scooping Sydney into his arms like a wriggling puppy.

"They're biting me!" she whimpered, still slapping at herself. "Vic, they're biting me!"

"Hang on, baby." Vic raced across the field, carrying her toward the horses I'd noticed earlier. For one crazy moment I thought he was planning to leap onto one of the beasts and ride off into the sunset like some demented cowboy. Instead, however, he headed straight over to the big water tank and dropped Sydney into it.

Water splashed out over the sides, and Sydney let out a squeak of surprise just before her head went under. "Good thinking," George said, watching along with the rest of us. "That's probably the quickest way to get them off her."

She was right. Within a moment or two, Sydney

was ant-free. Vic flicked a few ants off his own bare chest, then helped Sydney out of the water tank as the surprised horses looked on.

"What are you all waiting for?" he called irritably, glancing toward the rest of us. "Somebody get her a towel or something!"

"I'll go! I think there's a robe in the dressing room!" Deb called out.

"I'll come help you find it," Candy offered.

"What's Deb doing here?" George said in surprise as the two of them hurried off in the direction of the locker rooms. "I thought all us nonceleb bridesmaids were supposed to be off the hook for today."

I shrugged. Until that moment I hadn't noticed that Deb was there either. But the reason for her presence seemed like one of the least important questions of the moment.

Sydney was huddled up against Vic, shivering and dripping as the rest of us hurried over. "This is a nightmare," she moaned, staring tearfully at one of her arms. "They must've bitten me, like, a zillion times. And the bites are already starting to swell. Look!"

Sure enough, there were already several angry red welts standing out against her pale skin. "Whoa!" Bo said, staring at them. "What kind of psycho-freak ants were those?"

"She's got sensitive skin," Akinyi told him. "It

doesn't take much to make her swell up like crazy."

"That's right." Ellie was already examining the ant bites. "Oh, dear. I should call your father to see if we still have some of your allergy medicine—maybe that would help." Suddenly noticing that several camera operators were still filming, her face suddenly went stern. "Turn those cameras off right now!" she ordered.

At that moment Deb reappeared carrying a tube of something. "Look, we found some anti-itch stuff!" she said. "Candy's still back there looking for the robes. Here, let's put this on you before those bites get any worse."

"Cool," Vic said gratefully. "Hear that, baby? This stuff'll help."

"Thanks, Deb," Sydney said with a sniff. "But I think it's too late for that." Still, she stood there and allowed her friend to dab the cream onto her arms and shoulders.

Meanwhile Ellie Marvin was marching toward the closest cameraman, Mr. Bald-and-Bushy. "I said, turn those things off!" she said, shaking one finger in the man's face. "This isn't part of the deal, and my daughter doesn't need to be subjected to you people's sick curiosity and utter lack of human decency."

Hans Eberhart had been standing back watching the scene unfold with everyone else. Now he hurried forward. "Now, now, Mrs. Marvin," he said. "Let's not get upset. Remember, *Daredevils* is a reality show, eh? And so things like this will happen. After all, reality can be so incredibly . . . real, sometimes!"

Ellie glared at him. "Exactly what's so real about all this?" she demanded, waving an arm at the fake pyramids and palm trees.

Eberhart turned toward Vic and Sydney. "Please, Sydney," he said. "Can you explain to your dear mother about how reality TV works?"

Sydney sniffled. "Sorry, but this is all getting a little too *un*real for me," she said. "I need a moment. Excuse me, everyone."

Pulling away from Deb, who was still busily tending to her bites, she raced off toward the locker rooms. "Oh, dear," Donald murmured.

Eberhart just shrugged. "Take five, everyone," he called out, signaling for the cameras to stop rolling. He pointed to Mr. Bushy Eyebrows. "Butch, start setting up for the Egyptian sequence." As the cameraman nodded and strolled off toward the pyramid, the director turned toward Vic, Bo, and Dragon. "Boys, why don't you get dressed for that bit now? We can return to the Hawaiian business later."

Bo clapped Vic on the back. "Come on, bro," he said. "You heard the man. Let's get suited up pharaoh-style."

Vic looked vaguely mutinous for a moment as he stared after Sydney. Then he shrugged and sighed. "Fine," he said. Shooting a worried look at Akinyi, he added, "Call me if Syd needs me, okay?"

"Whatever." Akinyi, too, was staring anxiously after Sydney. "I'd better go check on her."

"Tell her I'll be right there, as soon as I give a piece of my mind to whoever was in charge of that lei," Ellie said grimly.

Her words snapped me back to the reality of the situation. Either River Heights had just been inflicted with a freak plague of biting ants . . . or the saboteur had struck again.

"I'm going to try to get a look at that lei," I whispered to Bess and George.

Bess nodded, glancing anxiously in the direction of the locker rooms. "Need our help?"

"Nope. Go check on Syd. I'll be there in a sec."

Bess and George hurried off. Eberhart had stepped forward to intercept Ellie, who was now ranting furiously at him. Just about everyone else was sort of drifting off, seeming uncertain what to do next.

I made a beeline for the fake beach. The wooden box was still standing open in the sand. Bending down, I saw that it was crawling with ants.

As I took a step backward, not wanting to risk getting bitten myself, I almost bumped into Donald.

"Oh, man," he exclaimed as he took a peek into the box, looking distressed. "I can't believe this. Poor Sydney!"

"I'm sure she'll be okay," I said automatically, more interested in looking around for the remains of the lei than in chatting with the PA. "And I'm sure it was just an unfortunate accident."

"It was no accident. I'm responsible!"

I blinked, glancing over at him. He'd straightened his thin shoulders, a grim look on his face.

"Huh?" I said. "Are you saying you put those ants on the lei?"

"Of course not!" Donald sounded insulted. "But I shouldn't have just left it sitting around unattended, where *anyone* could tamper with it." He shot a dark glance across the field.

Following his gaze, I saw Vic just disappearing into a trailer parked at the edge of the field. No one else was nearby, leading me to believe that the PA's gaze was definitely directed at the groom-to-be. Hmm, interesting . . .

Before I could fully process that, I realized that Donald was already gathering up the torn pieces of the white lei. For a second I almost told Donald why I wanted to look it over. But I decided against it. It seemed pretty unlikely that examining the lei would provide any useful clues to how the ants had gotten there.

"Excuse me," I said. "I think I'll go check on Sydney."

Leaving Donald muttering self-incriminations under his breath, I headed across the field to the locker room that was serving as a dressing room for Sydney and the other women on the set. I knocked and entered.

Sydney was sitting on a narrow bench in front of a mirror, dabbing at the corners of her eyes with a tissue. Akinyi, Deb, Candy, Bess, and George were all there too. Apparently Candy had found some bathrobes, because not only was Sydney now wrapped in one, but Candy was, too.

"Did they figure out where those icky things came from?" Candy demanded as soon as I entered, wrapping her arms around herself. The robe was a little big for her, so only her fingertips stuck out the ends of the sleeves. She shuddered from within the depths of the terry cloth. "I can't believe this happened. I hate bugs! If those things had been all over me, I would have died!"

Akinyi was slumped on a bench over by the sinks, still wearing her grass skirt and lei. "Okay, we get it," she said to Candy. "You've told us how much you hate bugs. This is about Syd, not you, remember?"

"Well, excuse me for having a phobia, Miss Perfect!" Candy huffed.

"Guys . . ." Bess began soothingly.

Deb looked up from her seat beside Sydney. She was still applying cream to Sydney's arm, pushing back the voluminous sleeve of the robe to do so.

"Oh, now, I know everyone's upset and all. But I'm sure it was just one of those things," she said in her cheerful way. "Everything will be all right."

Sydney sniffled. "I'm not so sure," she said, staring at her own red-eyed reflection in the mirror. "It was bad enough when my wedding was turning into a circus with this TV stuff. But now it's turning into a horror show!"

"There you go," Deb said, not seeming to be paying much attention to Sydney's words as she dabbed one last bit of cream on the back of her hand. "Now, let's get your face fixed up. Luckily you only got a couple of bites there—I'm sure we can cover those with makeup."

Just then a sharp whistle came from somewhere outside. "Sounds like they're starting the filming again," Candy said. "I'll go see what's happening. Somehow I don't think any of us are going to be ready for our close-ups anytime soon."

Akinyi shrugged. "I'll come with you."

George stared after them as they left together. "Wow," she said. "It's hard to tell whether those two are mad at each other or not."

Sydney smiled weakly. "Oh, they're always like

that," she said. Glancing at Deb, she added, "My makeup kit is out by the wardrobe trailer. Would you mind getting it?"

"You betcha," Deb said cheerfully, hurrying out.

As soon as she was gone, Sydney spun to face me. "Nancy, you've got to help me before everything is ruined!" she exclaimed. "I can't wait to marry Vic and spend the rest of my life with him. But if this wedding is going to be a disaster, I'd rather just elope and be done with it!"

"Hey, why not?" George put in brightly. "Eloping can be super romantic! All the excitement and I-do stuff without any of the lame speeches and bad dancing . . ."

"And bridesmaid dresses?" Bess put in, glaring at her. "You're not helping, George."

Sydney hardly seemed to hear them. She was still staring at me. "I just can't take this," she said. "It's not fair. I thought I was finished being scared after—"

"Here we are!" Deb sang out, rushing back in clutching a large metal box. A young woman I didn't know was right behind her. "And here's your makeup girl to work on your face."

I felt like grabbing Deb and the makeup artist and shoving them both back out the door. What had Sydney been about to say? Something in her eyes had suddenly reminded me of that weird moment at her house the other day when she'd told me about those threatening e-mails. Could there be something more to those, something she hadn't told me?

If so, it seemed she wasn't going to get the chance to fill me in anytime soon. Akinyi had just come back in as well, announcing that the boys were already filming the first part of the Egyptian traditions scene. Whatever that weird little moment had been, it was lost.

A little while later we were all out watching Vic, Bo, and Dragon clown around with some fake swords near the pyramid as the special effects director prepared for the next scene. Well, most of us were watching, anyway. Candy had developed a migraine and gone to lie down somewhere, and Ellie and Deb were in the dressing room helping Sydney get dressed and made up.

I found myself standing beside Akinyi, who was now dressed in her Egyptian costume. She looked stunning in it, though the effect was somewhat ruined by the worried crease in her brow.

"I can't believe this is happening," she said. "It's so unfair for poor Sydney."

I nodded, flashing back to my earlier speculation. Could Akinyi possibly be a suspect? "Yes," I agreed. "Things aren't going very well with her wedding so far."

"I know, the poor thing!" Akinyi shook her head. "I only hope she still doesn't have those hives for the big day. It's only a week away now, and everyone knows how sensitive her skin is."

"Really?" I said. "She's that sensitive, huh? I had no idea."

"Oh, yes, she's famous for it," Akinyi said. "She couldn't finish this one shoot last year because the foundation she was supposed to be showing made her break out." Just then there was a loud *whoosh* from nearby and Akinyi jumped, her eyes going wide as she clutched at her heart. "Oh, please. This is all too much!" she exclaimed. "Syd never should have agreed to get mixed up with this crazy show. Or even if she did, I should have known better than to get myself involved!"

I glanced over. The sound had been caused by a member of the special effects crew lighting a sort of blowtorch thing. They proceeded to use it to set the sword Bo was holding ablaze. He let out a cry of triumph and held the flaming sword aloft, waving it around over his head as the guy with the blowtorch headed for Dragon, who held out his own sword eagerly.

Akinyi was still moaning and griping, and I turned back to her, tut-tutting along as sympathetically as I could. However, I was feeling a little impatient. It would be a lot easier to get information out of Akinyi if she wasn't quite so quick to freak out over every little thing!

A sudden shriek jostled me out of such thoughts, making me jump right along with Akinyi. We both spun around as there was a flurry of shouts and exclamations. My eyes widened as I took in the scene.

Vic's hair was on fire!

FIRED UP

"Out of the way!" someone bellowed. "I've got him!" It was Butch, the bushy-browed cameraman. He dropped his camera and came barreling toward Vic, who was standing stock-still, seemingly in shock as the tips of his huge mass of black hair blazed.

Butch grabbed Vic around the waist. With three big steps, he was at the stock tank. He dunked Vic into the water headfirst.

All around, people were shouting and running around helplessly. But I relaxed as I saw a gush of steam come up from the water.

A moment later Butch yanked Vic up again by

the scruff of the neck. Vic came up sputtering and coughing.

"It's okay," the cameraman said, his moment of gallant action fading back into his usual gruff demeanor. "Fire's out."

He dropped Vic, who staggered and almost fell. But he caught himself and cautiously raised one hand to his head, as if wondering if it was still there.

"You all right, dude?" Bo shouted, racing over and pounding him on the back. "Did your head get burned?"

Pandora, too, rushed to Vic's side. "Oh, Vic!" she cried. "What happened?"

"Yes, what happened?" Eberhart said sternly.

The director glared at the special-effects guys as several paramedics rushed over and pushed Vic's friends out of their way. I'd vaguely noticed them earlier—George had said something about *Daredevils* always traveling with its own set of medics due to the risky nature of the stunts on the show. I was starting to see her point.

"Oh, oh," Akinyi was moaning, both hands covering her mouth as she stared at Vic in wide-eyed horror.

Leaving her to her meltdown, I hurried over to Bess and George, who were watching in shock nearby. "Whoa," George breathed as I joined them. "Did you see that?"

"Lucky that camera guy was so quick to react," Bess said. "Lucky Vic has so much hair, too. I think the fire was out before it even had a chance to reach his scalp." She glanced over at Vic, now completely surrounded by paramedics, and bit her lip. "I hope so, anyway," she added softly.

"How did the fire start?" I asked. "I was looking away when it happened."

George shrugged. "Not sure," she said. "The guy lit Vic's sword, and when he started waving it around like the other guys, the flames just seemed to jump right into his hair."

Meanwhile the special effects director was talking to Eberhart. "It shouldn't have happened," the guy insisted, seeming shaken. "I'm telling you, we followed all the safety procedures. It shouldn't have happened!"

"But it did," Eberhart barked at him. "And I want to know why."

"Yeah," I murmured, more to myself than my friends. "You and me both."

Vic was incredibly lucky. He ended up with some first-degree burns on his head, face, and arms, but nothing more. Of course, his hair was another story. It was going to be a while before he'd be able to sport his trademark long spikes again. But all things considered, that didn't seem like a very big deal. The paramedics wanted to send him to the hospital just in case, but Vic refused to go.

"I didn't go to the hospital when I fell halfway down the St. Louis Arch during *Daredevils*," he boasted, already back to at least eighty percent of his usual bravado. "And I'm not going for this!"

Bo clapped him on the back. "Way to be, bro!"

Meanwhile the special-effects guys, one of the paramedics, and a few other members of the crew were huddled nearby. They'd clipped off a charred bit of Vic's hair to examine in search of answers to what had happened. Finally the main special effects guy marched over to Eberhart, looking grim.

"We've figured it out," he announced. He jabbed a finger toward Vic. "He used the wrong hair gel! We told you everyone had to stick to water-based products for this stunt, but there's definitely traces of that flammable goop he usually uses."

Vic overheard and hurried over. "Yo, I used that new water-based stuff," he said. "I remember, because the whole time I was getting ready I was thinking it wasn't as lame as I expected—worked just as well as my usual stuff, actually. Even smelled the same."

"Are you wacked, dude?" Dragon snorted, touching his own carefully coiffed, though much shorter, spikes. "That water-based junk stank like flowers or something. Almost made me gag!"

Pandora smiled. "Aw, I thought it smelled great," she said. "Much better than that petroleum nightmare Vic's always slathering all over his head."

Vic looked confused. "I didn't smell flowers. But I'm sure I used the new stuff. Light blue jar, right?"

"That's the stuff," a woman called out. "I put a fresh jar on everyone's dressing table as soon as we set up this morning."

"Are you certain you didn't grab your old gel by mistake?" Eberhart asked Vic.

"Positive, man!" Vic insisted, wincing as a paramedic came over to dab something on one of his burns. "I didn't even see the other tube on the table."

Eberhart pointed to Donald, who was hovering near the back of the crowd. "Go check Vic's dressing table," he ordered. "See what hair gel is there."

"Yes, sir," Donald said, scurrying off.

"Why are they blaming Vic for this, anyway?" George wondered aloud to me and Bess. "I thought all these TV people had people to do their hair and makeup."

Pandora was close enough to overhear. "Not Vic!" she said with a laugh, glancing at us. "He's fine with other people dealing with his face and wardrobe. But his hair is his baby—he always does that himself."

"I'm telling you guys, I used the right gel!" Vic was still protesting as several other people started talking at once. "I'm not a total idiot, you know!"

"We know, dude. But this wouldn't be the first time you got so ADD-distracted in the middle of a shoot that you mixed things up." Bo chortled and shot a look at Pandora. "Hey, remember the time we were supposed to eat those fish heads in Alaska, and he got himself so psyched up that he ate the fish-shaped piece of cardboard the camera people stuck on the plate to check the lighting?"

Pandora laughed. "Yeah. And what about when we were supposed to ride that zip line across the Grand Canyon? Good thing someone noticed he'd grabbed the wrong gloves before his turn came, or he'd probably be splattered all over the bottom of the Colorado River right now."

The stories seemed to lighten the mood a bit. Several members of the crew piped in with anecdotes of their own, and soon even Vic was laughing.

But I wasn't paying much attention to the stories. I was much more focused on this latest disaster. Sure, it was possible that this was an innocent mistake, that Vic had grabbed the wrong hair gel without noticing. But given everything else that had been happening lately, I wasn't counting on it.

Soon Donald came running back, accompanied by a couple of young women who appeared to be part of the makeup crew. "We searched everywhere!" Donald said breathlessly. "Vic's usual hair gel isn't anywhere in the dressing rooms."

"See? Told you!" Vic exclaimed.

"Wait!" Donald waved his hands. "That's not all— there's a jar of the water-based stuff on Vic's table. But it's still sealed. Nobody's used it."

Vic's triumphant expression changed to one of confusion. "What are you talking about?" he said. "Of course I used it. This doesn't just happen, you know." He raised one hand to touch his spikes, though he looked crestfallen when he remembered they weren't there anymore. "Anyway, I definitely used *something* in a blue jar to do my hair."

Pandora shrugged. "Maybe he used Dragon's jar."

"No way." Dragon shook his head. "Mine was sealed when Jana opened it to do my hair. After she was done, I accidentally knocked it off the table and the jar broke, so we tossed it."

Bo ran a hand over his blond buzz cut, which was way to short too require any sort of styling product. "Well, he certainly didn't borrow mine," he joked.

Vic smiled weakly. "Whatever," he said. "Maybe someone tossed mine, too."

"Or maybe someone tossed your tube of Fabulous and Flammable," Pandora put in.

Vic scowled at her. "I'm telling you, I used the right gel!"

Pandora raised both hands in a gesture of surrender. "Chill, dude. It was a joke. Did the fire burn away your sense of humor, too?"

"Come on," I murmured to my friends. "Let's go sniff around a little while everyone's still distracted."

We slipped away from the rest of the group. "What are we looking for?" George asked. "Donald said they already checked Vic's dressing room."

"I bet they didn't check every trash bin in the stadium," I said. "If Vic is telling the truth about what happened, it sounds like someone switched out the water-based gel with his usual flammable stuff—probably even put it in the other container, knowing what was likely to happen."

Bess's eyes widened. "Ooh, nasty!"

"Exactly," I said grimly. "Which is why we need to find the evidence. We have to get to the bottom of things before whoever's doing this escalates things even more and somebody gets really hurt, like—"

"Sydney!" George blurted out.

I glanced ahead, realizing Sydney had just emerged from the locker room area with her mother and Deb right behind her. In all the excitement, I'd forgotten that she was still holed up getting ready.

She looked gorgeous dressed as an Egyptian princess, even with a long scarf draped around her neck and chest to hide the ant bites. But her expression was distraught. "This is a disaster!" she cried as soon as she spotted us.

For a second I thought someone must have already told her what had happened to Vic. But then I saw that she was clutching her green-beaded PDA. She held it up in front of us.

"I just got a text from River Street Blossoms and Bows," she wailed. "Someone just canceled the entire flower order for the wedding!"

9

FOOD FOR THOUGHT

After what had happened to Vic, a canceled flower order seemed pretty minor. But it was obvious that it had Sydney on the edge of a breakdown.

"It'll be okay," Bess said, hurrying over and putting an arm around her. "My mom knows Mrs. Rayne over at Blossoms and Bows pretty well. I'm sure if we just call her and explain . . ."

"That's what I've been telling her," Ellie Marvin agreed, sounding exasperated. "This isn't the end of the world, Sydney."

"Maybe not." Sydney sniffled. "But it's just one

more disaster in the larger disaster that my wedding is becoming!"

Akinyi came hurrying toward us, arriving just in time to hear the last part of what Sydney had said. "Oh, so you heard about Vic's hair?" she exclaimed. "I can't believe it! Thank goodness he wasn't burned more seriously."

"What?" Sydney blinked. "Vic's hair? Burned? What are you talking about, Kinnie?"

I winced. This was the last straw Sydney needed to make her go back to her earlier plan to elope. "Everyone's okay now," I said quickly. "Don't worry."

Sydney hardly seemed to hear me, demanding that Akinyi explain what she was talking about. Sure enough, as soon as she heard about the fire, she freaked out, bursting into tears and threatening once more to call off the wedding.

Luckily Donald arrived on the scene at that moment. Upon hearing the latest problem, he immediately whipped out his cell phone and called the flower shop.

"There, that's all fixed," he announced as he hung up a few minutes later. "They hadn't even canceled the order with their supplier yet—they wanted to double-check first. So no harm done."

Sydney sniffled. "Thanks, Donald," she said. "I guess we're down to one disaster for today after all.

Now if you'll all excuse me, I need to go check on poor Vic."

"So Vic convinced her to relax and keep going ahead with the wedding?" Ned Nickerson asked.

I glanced over at him. We were at a quiet table at our favorite Italian restaurant. Ned and I had been a couple for years. But just recently, we'd started a new tradition: Friday date night. We'd been forced to spend way too much time apart a month or two earlier, and that had made us realize we needed to set aside time for each other and stick to it no matter what.

"Yep," I said, reaching for my water glass. "It's kind of amazing. Vic comes across as this totally hyper, larger-than-life, spastic type of character. But he seems to be the only one who can calm Sydney down when she gets really worked up."

"Love is an amazing thing," Ned said lightly, winking at me in the candlelight. "So do you have any suspects yet in the case?"

I sighed. "A whole slew of them. Unfortunately, none of them are too convincing." Tapping my fingers on the tablecloth, I thought over the cast of characters involved in the wedding. "There's the TV director for one."

"Hans Eberhart?" Ned said. "Do you really think

he'd do something like that? He's pretty well-known—would he really risk his reputation that way?"

I shrugged. "I'm not sure. George seems to think he might harbor a grudge because he doesn't have the kind of respected, artsy career he should have had after his early success. He could be trying to get that career back on track. Or even just trying to get the show higher ratings."

"I guess." Ned spun a bite of his pasta on his fork, looking somewhat unconvinced. "Who else have you got?"

"I hate to say it, but there's Sydney herself. Could she be having second thoughts about filming her wedding and be trying to sabotage it?" I smiled wryly as Ned glanced up from his food in surprise. "I know, I know. I can't really believe she'd be capable of some of this stuff either. Especially since Vic almost got badly hurt twice now—first by the jet fuel thing, and now the fire." I pursed my lips thoughtfully. "But I have a definite hunch that there's something she isn't telling me about all this. And that makes me wonder."

Ned still looked skeptical. "Okay," he said. "Anyone else?"

I picked up my garlic bread and stared at it. "Well, I can't help noticing that Syd's friend Deb always seems to be close at hand when things go wrong. She refused the jet fuel–laced drink at the party, and she turned up at the filming this morning even though she wasn't supposed to be there as far as I know."

"Deb?" Ned echoed. "Wait, are you talking about the Deb who works at the Pop In and Shop? You think she could be doing all this?"

"Maybe. What if she's envious of her old friend's beauty and success?" I set down the garlic bread without taking a bite, thinking over everything I knew about Deb Camden. "Come to think of it, she's mentioned she doesn't have much money—that's why she's working at the convenience store, to put herself through school. Could there be some kind of motive there?"

Ned shrugged. "Anything's possible," he said. "You've certainly busted less likely suspects before. But listen, what about this Vic guy himself? Is he on your list? Because based on what you've told me, he makes a lot of sense as a suspect."

"What do you mean?"

Ned put down his fork and starting ticking things off on his fingers. "He could have sent those e-mails. He had access to the invitations. He was the one who 'discovered' the jet fuel before anyone drank it."

"He was the one who hung that lei around Syd's neck," I went on, nodding slowly. "And he's the one who may have used the wrong hair gel, whether accidentally or not." I shuddered. "But would anyone really be nuts enough to light his own hair on fire?"

"You said the show always has medics standing by, right?" Ned pointed out. "Vic would know that too—he'd have to be pretty sure he wouldn't be too badly injured." He cracked a smile. "Besides, I've seen the show. It certainly wouldn't be the first time he'd put himself in serious harm's way. That guy is nuts just to have done half the things he did on there!"

"You have a point," I agreed, smiling ruefully in return. "But what's his motive? He really seems to adore Sydney—why would he hurt her like this?"

"The dude seems to crave attention, and this is getting him plenty. Maybe he's not really thinking about the rest."

"Okay, but if you want to look at it that way, it seems just as likely that one of the other Daredevils could be behind it," I said. "Especially that Dragon guy—he's not even that close to Vic, and George is sure that Dragon thinks his stint on *Daredevils* will jump-start a showbiz career. And then of course with Pandora there's the whole love-triangle thing. Maybe she's trying to break up the wedding to get Vic back for herself."

"Maybe," Ned agreed. "But would she really put her beloved in mortal danger not once but twice?"

I shrugged. "Like you said, she'd know as well as

anyone that the hair gel thing probably wouldn't be too serious. But maybe that does make her a less likely suspect for the PowerUp prank. That easily could have killed him, and several other people too." Thinking about the jet fuel incident reminded me of one more name to add to the suspect list. "Then there's Akinyi," I said. "She refused to join in on the PowerUp toast. And she was pretty quick to tell Syd what happened with Vic's hair today—almost like she *wanted* her to freak out. Besides that, she definitely knew that Syd has sensitive skin and would be more affected than most people by those ant bites."

"Why would she want to bust up Sydney's wedding?" Ned asked. "I thought they were best friends."

"Me too," I said. "But I guess she could be nursing some kind of grudge we don't know about. Oh! Or maybe it has to do with Josh somehow." I quickly told Ned about Akinyi's screenwriter boyfriend. "I just remembered, one of the ideas Josh was telling Eberhart about had something to do with a deadly swarm of bugs! Sounds awfully similar to what happened with those ants. . . . What if he's behind this? Or he and Akinyi are doing it all together?"

"Okay, they would definitely have the means and the opportunity," Ned said. "But again I ask— why? Where's the motive?"

I slumped in my seat, playing with the edge of my napkin. "I have no idea," I admitted. "Professional jealousy? Or maybe some kind of personal vendetta we don't know about yet?"

"Sounds pretty weak."

"Yeah," I agreed. "Definitely weak. But you know me. I'm not giving up until I figure it out."

The next day was Saturday, exactly one week before the wedding. It was also the day of Sydney's bridal shower. Sydney's parents' home was only a few blocks from mine, so my friends and I walked over there together.

"I wish I was going on that retreat instead of to this stupid shower," George muttered, picking at the waistband of the sundress she'd borrowed from me.

Bess slapped her hands away. "Leave that alone," she ordered. "It's perfect. And stop complaining. You know you wouldn't have any more fun at some silly all-male 'retreat' out in the woods somewhere."

I grinned at the expression on George's face, which said she wasn't too sure about that. But she didn't bother to argue the point.

Vic and the rest of the guys had headed off that morning to the state park a few miles downriver for a day of male bonding. I wasn't clear on all the details, but I suspected there might be some banging of drums and pounding of chests involved.

In any case, the whole world would be able to check out those details soon enough. Eberhart and most of the film crew had gone with them to film the whole thing, leaving behind Madge, Donald, and a handful of camera operators and others to record the shower.

"So did Vic's family arrive safely last night?" I asked as we walked.

George nodded. "Sydney talked to him right after they got here," she said. "His mom and his three cousins who are going to be groomsmen came, along with a couple of others, I think. The rest aren't flying in until next week."

We were almost to the Marvin house by then. "I hope Sydney can manage to relax and enjoy herself today," Bess said as we headed up the front steps. "She was really upset yesterday."

"Can you blame her?" George rolled her eyes. "Her fiancé almost spontaneously combusted."

"Hush," I warned, raising my hand to the doorbell. "We're here."

The door burst open a moment later, revealing Pandora. "Hi, guys!" she gushed. "Come on in—the other bridesmaids and family are all here. We're just trying to get everything set up before the rest of the guests arrive."

I felt a bit underdressed beside Pandora's outfit, an elaborate Indian sari. Seeing Akinyi and Candy didn't chase that feeling away. Akinyi looked taller, thinner, and more exotic than ever in a form-fitting modern strapless orange gown and four-inch heels, while Candy was attired in a Victorian-inspired pale-blue gown complete with totally impractical elbow-length white silk gloves.

Luckily, however, everyone else looked much more normal. Sydney was stylish and pretty in a long-sleeved dress with a patterned silk scarf draped artfully around her neck to cover most of her ant bites. Ellie, Deb, and the other locals were dressed in outfits similar to what my friends and I were wearing.

Ellie bustled up to greet us and introduce us to Vic's mother, who was helping Deb fold napkins in the kitchen. Tina Valdez was small and thin, with gray-streaked dark hair pulled back into a tight bun. She seemed to be as quiet and unassuming as her son was brash and in-your-face.

"Nice to meet you, Mrs. Valdez," Bess said. "You must be very proud of your son."

"Oh, yes." The woman flashed us an uncertain smile as her eyes darted around the room. "Our whole family is proud of Vic. I just don't know what to make of all this TV business sometimes, you know?"

"I can only imagine!" Deb put in with a giggle. "Still, it must be terribly exciting having a celebrity in the family. Like living the lifestyle of the rich and famous!"

"I'm sure that's very nice," Ellie put in, sounding slightly disapproving. "But the most important thing is family, isn't that right, Tina?"

"Isn't what right?" Sydney asked, hurrying in. "Is everything almost done in here? They just turned on the cameras, and the rest of the guests should be here soon."

"We're just about ready," Ellie told her. "Just waiting for one last delivery from the bakery."

Just then there was a knock on the back door. I hurried over to open it and found fifteen-year-old Mary Mackin standing there. Mary's parents own one of the best bakeries in River Heights.

"Oh, good," I said with a smile. "We were waiting for you."

"Hi, Nancy," Mary greeted me cheerfully. She held up a large white bakery box tied with string. "Sorry this is late. It took us a while to make up a new batch of cupcakes after the last-minute change in the order."

"Thanks, Mary," I said, glancing down at the order slip that was stuck into the string on top of the box. "I'll take care of them."

I carried the box over to the table, where Sydney, her mother, George, Tina Valdez, and Deb were just finishing up with the napkins. "Is that the bakery delivery, Nancy?" Ellie asked.

"Yep," I said, setting down the box. "Two dozen double-chocolate cupcakes with fudge frosting."

"Yum, chocolate cupcakes," George said hungrily.

But Sydney just stared at the box—and then burst into tears.

CAKE MISTAKE

"**W**hat's the matter?" I exclaimed, startled. "Sydney, what is it?"

"*Chocolate* cupcakes?" Sydney wailed. "But I'm allergic to chocolate! That's why I *specifically* ordered yellow cupcakes with vanilla frosting!"

"Oh, dear! Maybe the tag is wrong." Deb quickly opened the box and peeked inside. "Nope, they're chocolate all right. But don't worry, Syd—I'll run out and buy some vanilla ones somewhere if you want."

Sydney was already regaining control of herself. "No, that's all right," she said with one last sniffle, grabbing a napkin to wipe her eyes. "Sorry, I guess the stress is getting to me. Of course this is no big deal. It's not like I have to eat the cupcakes myself for my guests to enjoy them."

"That's right," Ellie said firmly. "Now, Sydney, pull yourself together. George, Bess, take the napkins out to the sideboard. Deb, grab the coffee urn and put that out too. Tina, if you wouldn't mind helping Nancy bring the coffee cups . . ."

We all obeyed her orders, scurrying around the kitchen. Just then Candy came hurrying in.

"People are starting to arrive," she said. "Where's the guest of honor? Come on, Syd—get out there and let's get this party started!"

"We're almost ready," Ellie said. "Candy, be a dear and put those cupcakes on that tray over there, all right?"

Candy blinked, staring from the open box of fudge-frosted cupcakes to the empty silver tray nearby. "Um, can someone else do it?" she said. "These gloves are way hard to get on and off, and I don't want to stain them."

Ellie frowned, her eyes flashing with irritation. I was afraid the stress was getting to her, too. She looked just about ready to snap—and that was the last thing Sydney needed.

"I'll do it," I offered, shoving the cups I was holding into Candy's gloved hands. "Here, you carry these."

That did the trick. The others hurried out to the

living room, and I quickly stacked the cupcakes on the tray. But my mind was elsewhere—namely, over at the Mackins' bakery. Mary had said something about a last-minute change in the cupcake order. Who had made that change? I wished I'd thought to ask her. Making a mental note to call and ask as soon as I got the chance, I picked up the loaded tray and headed out to join the party.

The bridal shower proceeded smoothly for the next hour or two. At first most of the guests were a bit giggly and self-conscious about the TV cameras. But they soon relaxed into the event, and even I mostly forgot the cameras were there after a while. Madge was staying out of the way, sitting in the kitchen drinking cup after cup of coffee and occasionally stepping outside to make a phone call. Donald quickly won over the girls and women at the shower with his helpfulness and good cheer as he bustled back and forth refilling the coffee urn and bringing out more food. The camera operators themselves were as discreet as possible, staying mostly in the background.

"I doubt they'll use much of this footage," George murmured to me at one point. "Who wants to watch a bunch of ladies sitting around sipping tea? That's why they sent all the senior peeps out on the retreat with the guys."

"You're the expert on reality TV," I replied with a smile. "I'll take your word for it. But all I can say is some people might be awfully disappointed if their fancy outfits end up on the cutting room floor." I shot a look at Akinyi, Candy, and Pandora.

A few minutes later Ellie clapped her hands and announced that it was time to open the gifts. Sydney blushed, but obediently came forward and took a seat in the middle of the room.

"You guys really didn't have to get me anything," she insisted as Deb and Bess started piling beautifully wrapped boxes at her feet. "Getting to marry Vic is the only gift I ever wanted."

"Boo!" Pandora called out playfully. "Are you crazy, girl? Go for the loot!"

That made everyone laugh, including Sydney. "Well, thanks," she said. "Now, let's see what we have here. . . ."

She started unwrapping, with everyone oohing and aahing over each gift she revealed. There was a huge stack of them, including some from friends and family who couldn't attend the wedding. There were also packages from Sydney's modeling agency and several of Vic's other costars.

Despite her protests, it was obvious that Sydney was having a good time, like a little kid on Christmas morning. She exclaimed happily over each and every offering, from the agency's elaborate gourmet food basket to a handmade beaded necklace from her six-year-old cousin.

"Okay, what's next?" Deb said, digging through the remaining pile for another gift. "Hmm, this one looks interesting—but there's no card."

Sydney took the small, plainly wrapped box Deb was holding. She turned it over in her hands. "Maybe the card's inside," she said. "Or it might have fallen off in the pile. Is it from someone here?" She glanced around the room, but nobody fessed up.

"Just open it," Akinyi urged. "It looks like jewelry!"

Sydney smiled and obeyed, carefully sliding off the ribbon and removing the paper. When she lifted the lid off the box inside, Deb leaned over her shoulder for a better look.

"Oh, it's beautiful!" she cried, grabbing the box out of Sydney's hand and holding it up so everyone could get a look at the contents. "See? It's one of those silhouette necklaces!"

Nestled into the box was a Victorian-style cameo on a slender gold chain. "Nice," Bess commented approvingly. "Definitely Sydney's style."

"Oh, isn't it gorgeous?" Pandora exclaimed as most of the other guests oohed and aahed. "But I wonder who it's from?"

I glanced at Sydney, who hadn't said anything since opening the box. She was staring at the necklace, white-faced and looking oddly shaken. When I shifted my gaze to Ellie, I saw that she, too, seemed startled by the gift. Once again I flashed back to those odd moments when I felt they weren't telling me everything.

"Excuse me," I said, standing up and stepping over to Ellie. "Could I steal you for a sec? I think the coffee's running low and I'm not sure where the filters are."

It was a lame excuse, but it seemed to work—at least, nobody spared us a glance as I dragged Ellie out to the kitchen and shut the door behind us. Fortunately Madge and Donald were nowhere in sight at the moment and we had the place to ourselves. Ellie sank down onto a chair, staring into space with a furrowed brow, hardly seeming to notice me standing there.

"Okay, what's going on?" I asked her urgently. "Why did you and Syd look so weird as soon as she opened that gift? Is there something you're not telling me? Because I need to know everything if I'm supposed to help get to the bottom of this!"

Ellie blinked and glanced at me. She frowned, and for a second I thought she was going to get angry about me grilling her like that.

Then she sighed, seeming to deflate. "Oh, I suppose you're right; I'd better tell you," she said. "It's not that we wanted to keep things from you, Nancy, and we do appreciate all your help with this. It's just that Sydney simply wanted to forget. . . ." She sighed again and closed her eyes for a moment. Then, opening them, she looked up at me. "You see, Sydney used to have a stalker."

"A stalker? What do you mean—like a crazed fan?"

Ellie nodded. "Something like that. He contacted her online and wouldn't leave her alone—insisted that the two of them were destined to be together and so forth. He used to e-mail and text her dozens of times a day."

"Yikes," I said. "So who was he?"

"We never did find out his real name," Ellie said. "Online, he went by the name MrSilhouette."

"Weird handle," I commented.

"He claimed it was supposed to symbolize his relation to Sydney—something about always being in the shadows of her life."

"Creepy."

She nodded. "Then again, maybe he was just saying that," she said. "The name might just as easily have come from his bald head. He seemed weirdly proud of his own silhouette, so to speak—even sent

Sydney a photo of the back of his head once when she demanded to know who he was."

"So you were never able to ID him?" I asked. "Not even from that photo?"

Ellie shook her head. "Your father did all he could to help. So did the NYPD and the private detective her agency hired. But MrSilhouette caught on to the investigation and dropped out of sight. Hasn't bothered her since." She shot a glance in the direction of the party and bit her lip. "At least until now . . ."

I widened my eyes as the first part of what she'd said sank in. So *that* was the business Dad had been helping Sydney with last year!

"So you think that necklace came from this MrSilhouette?" I asked.

"It can't be a coincidence, can it?"

I shrugged. As Bess had mentioned, the cameo necklace was a beautiful piece of jewelry that had that classic Sydney style. It might have been chosen by anyone. But how likely was that given what I'd just learned?

Not very likely, I thought grimly.

Just then Madge came in from her latest phone call. Ellie excused herself and hurried back out to check on Sydney and I followed more slowly, my head spinning with what she'd told me.

What did this mean for my case? Could the mysterious MrSilhouette be behind all the trouble? If so, where was he—and *who* was he?

I took the first opportunity to pull Bess and George aside to discuss it. We huddled in the front hallway, talking in whispers. I quickly told them what I'd just learned from Ellie.

"Whoa," George said. "So do you think that's our guy?"

"I'm not sure," I admitted, rubbing my forehead as if that might jump-start my brain and help me figure it out. "I mean, it's certainly possible he sent that cameo. But even if he did, we shouldn't necessarily assume he did the other stuff."

"How could he have?" Bess leaned back against the front door. "I mean, like we keep saying, anyone could have sent those e-mails. . . ."

"Or changed that bakery order," George added. "Or canceled the flowers."

"Or called the police with that false tip about the plane," I finished. "But what about the other stuff? The jet fuel, the hair gel, the ants—all that took place on closed sets."

Bess nodded. "Right. A stranger couldn't have made it past security."

"Which leads us right back to where we were before," I said. "MrSilhouette or no MrSilhouette, whoever's doing this isn't a stranger. It has to be someone involved in the production. But who?"

We ran quickly over the options. Was Eberhart trying to pump up his career with some invented "reality"? Was Pandora trying to break up the wedding and steal Vic for herself? Could one of the other reality contestants be getting back at Vic for something or striking out due to his greater fame? Was one of the models trying to sabotage Sydney out of professional jealousy or for some other reason? Could Sydney or her mother be trying to back out of the wedding show? Was Deb trying to gain more importance in Sydney's life by creating these disasters and then helping her through them?

"Okay, that's a lot of suspects," George said uncertainly. "But a thought just occurred to me. Would all of them know about Syd's chocolate allergy?"

"I don't know," I said. "A lot of people seemed to know about her sensitive skin, at least according to Akinyi."

"Ooh! I just thought of something else," Bess said. "What if someone on the crew is actually MrSilhouette? That one cameraman is bald— what's his name? Butch, I think."

"I suppose it's possible." I sighed. "We might as well add him to the list with everybody else."

"There are just too many suspects with too many possible motives," George said in frustration. "But none of them seem like a slam dunk—or even particularly plausible."

"I know." I kicked at the corner of the foyer's Persian rug. "It's driving me crazy. Plus we don't even know for sure that they're all connected. Some could just be normal wedding craziness, and others could be the result of a risk-taking show like *Daredevils* or—"

I was interrupted by a sudden burst of tinny music. "What's that?" George said, patting the nonexistent pocket of her dress. "Is that someone's phone?"

"Not mine," Bess said, checking her purse.

"There it is." A PDA with a familiar green-beaded skin was lying on the foyer's tasteful mahogany bench half-covered by someone's sweater. "Hey, that's Syd's phone," I added. "I wonder if she knows she left it there."

I grabbed it, planning to take it back out to Sydney in the other room. But the beaded skin was more slippery than I was expecting, and I almost dropped it.

"Oops!" I said as my finger slipped, pressing a button with a loud beep. "Uh-oh, I hope I didn't, like, erase anything important. . . ."

I glanced at the screen. A text message had just popped up there, probably due to my accidental button-pushing. Normally I wouldn't have read Sydney's private message, of course. But the first

line of this one caught my eye, and I gasped as I
scanned the rest:

CAN'T U TAKE A HINT?
U & VIC R AS DIFFRNT AS CHOC AND VANILLA
BETTER GET SOME COLD FEET B4 IT'S 2 LATE!

PARTY TALK

Bess and George heard me gasp and came over to read the text over my shoulder. "Chocolate and vanilla!" Bess exclaimed. "Do you think that's a reference to the mix-up with the cupcakes?"

"Has to be. And that means it was probably sent by someone right here at this party," I said grimly. I shoved the PDA at George. "Take this. I want to get back out there and see who could have sent it."

I hurried back into the main room, scanning the guests. Unfortunately, I soon realized that the only person I could definitely cross off the suspect list was Akinyi. She wasn't carrying a purse, and there was no way she could hide so much as a Band-Aid in her tight dress, let alone a cell phone. Plus she was still sitting exactly where I'd last seen her with one high-heeled shoe kicked off.

But nearly anyone else could have done it. People were milling around from room to room, and most of the women were carrying purses. It wouldn't be difficult for any of them to slip off just long enough to send that text.

Bess came up behind me. "Are you sure it was someone here?" she asked quietly. "Someone from the guys' retreat could have called the bakery and then sent that text once enough time had passed to be sure the cupcakes had arrived."

"Good point." I bit my lip, realizing that text message might not be quite as revealing as I'd hoped. "But I thought the retreat was supposed to be some kind of back-to-nature caveman thing? Were they allowed to bring cell phones?"

Bess shrugged. "There's Donald." She pointed to the PA, who had just emerged from the kitchen with a new tray of hors d'oeuvres. "He might know."

I hurried over. "Hi, Nancy," Donald greeted me with a smile. "Shrimp?" He held up his tray.

I waved it off. "No thanks," I said. "Listen, I have a question. What's the deal with the guys' retreat? Do you think they have their cell phones with them?"

"Well, they're not supposed to," Donald replied, tossing his sandy brown bangs off his forehead. "The idea is that they're meant to leave all modern stuff behind and get in touch with their authentic nature, or something like that." He waved his free hand dismissively. "But knowing those guys, I wouldn't be at all surprised if most of them sneaked a cell or a laptop along anyway." He grimaced slightly. "It would probably kill most of them to go an entire day without checking their own press."

I chuckled politely. "Okay, thanks," I said, feeling a flash of sympathy for him. It seemed as if he really did have a pretty thankless job most of the time.

Then again, his job also means he's almost always around, with lots of access to everyone and everything having to do with this production, I mused as Donald turned away to offer his canapés to a passing guest. *If anyone could've pulled off most of this mischief without breaking a sweat, it's him. But what possible motive could he have? I doubt he'd resort to attempted murder just because he thinks Vic's kind of a stuck-up jerk. . . .*

In any case, I seemed to be right back where I'd started. The text message could have come from anyone on the suspect list. So what now?

Remembering that I still hadn't called the bakery to see who had changed the order, I decided I might as well do that now. I'd set down my purse somewhere with my phone in it, so rather than wasting time looking for it, I headed into the kitchen to use the phone there.

The kitchen was deserted when I got there. But as I headed for the phone, I heard someone push through the door behind me. Turning, I saw that it was Akinyi.

"Nancy, I'm glad I caught you alone," she said, tottering toward me on her high heels. "Listen, you have to figure out this mystery soon! Otherwise I'm afraid poor Sydney is going off the deep end for sure!"

I was taken aback. "Solve the—wait, you mean you know I'm a detective?"

Akinyi shrugged. "Of course," she said matter-of-factly. "Sydney tells me everything. In fact, I'm probably the only one here who knows just how hard it was for Syd not to flip out when she got that horrible silhouette necklace! Oh, and Candy, too, of course—she was around for some of that mess as well. . . ."

"Oh," I said, still too surprised to respond otherwise. "Um, well, I'm trying my best."

"Good. Let me know if I can do anything to help." With that, Akinyi turned and hurried back out.

I just stood there for a moment, my mind clicking away with what I'd just learned. Then, realizing that I probably wouldn't have the kitchen to myself for long, I did what I'd come to do—called the bakery.

"Sure, Nancy," Mrs. Mackin said once she'd heard my question. "I took that message myself. It came just an hour before the party via text message."

I thanked her and hung up. Oh well. That hadn't narrowed things down much. . . .

Just then the door opened again. This time Sydney herself came in. "Oh! Hi, Nancy," she said. "One of the camera guys needs to talk to Madge. Have you seen her?"

"She must be outside on the phone," I said distractedly. "But listen, Sydney. I have a question for you. Exactly how and where did you first meet Vic?"

Sydney blinked, seeming a bit perplexed by the sudden change of topic. "Um, it was at a dinner party back in New York," she said. "At Candy's apartment."

"Yes?" I urged.

Sydney smiled, her eyes taking on a distant glow as she recounted the rest of the story. "There were just six of us there," she said. "Me, Candy, Akinyi, Vic, Bo, and Josh. Candy had met the two *Daredevils* guys at a club the weekend before and thought they were a lot of fun, so she decided to have them over. Being in a small group like that gave me and Vic a chance to get to know each other pretty quickly. . . ." She sighed happily. "And I guess you could say the rest was history."

It was sweet to see that, even with all the trouble and trauma revolving around this wedding, she was clearly still thrilled to be preparing to marry her dream guy. But I didn't have time to linger on that. Another piece of the puzzle had just clicked into place in my mind.

"Excuse me," I said as Madge wandered in from outside and a couple of guests came from the living room looking for clean spoons. "I'll talk to you later, okay?"

I hurried back out to the living room in search of a more private phone. Not wanting to waste time searching for my cell, I grabbed George by the arm and asked to borrow hers.

"You have unlimited long distance, right?" I asked as I hurried out into the foyer, already dialing information. "Because this might take a couple of calls. . . ."

"Well?" George demanded when I hung up a few minutes later. "Find out anything interesting?"

"Very." I smiled, then turned and hurried back out to join the party. Explanations could come later. I didn't want to let the chance to prove my theory slip away.

The party was still in full swing. I wound my way through the crowd, making a beeline for the tray of fudgy chocolate cupcakes on the table nearest the kitchen. Choosing the biggest, gooiest one from the pile, I picked it up and then wandered across the busy room, looking for a certain person. . . .

"Oops!" I cried out as my foot caught on the rug and I went flying.

LOOSE ENDS

"Oh, I'm so sorry!" I cried as I stopped myself from falling by grabbing on to Candy. In the process, the cupcake I was holding ended up smeared all over her long, white silk gloves.

"Hey!" Candy exclaimed, staggering backward and almost falling herself. Then she glanced at her gloves and her eyes widened. "Oh no, look what you did! They're ruined!"

"I'm so sorry," I said again. "It's all my fault. Please, let me take those gloves—I'll have them dry-cleaned for you. I'm sure the chocolate will come out."

Candy pulled her arms in toward herself. "Never

mind, it's okay," she said. "No big deal—it was just an accident, right?"

"Please, I insist," I said, making no effort to keep my voice down. By now some of the other party-goers were drifting toward us, looking curious.

"Oh, dear." Ellie hurried forward for a look. "That's quite a mess. But Nancy is right—a good dry cleaner can set them right again."

I nodded earnestly. "If you give them to me right now, I can run them right over to New Street—the dry cleaning shop there does a fabulous job. They'll probably be good as new before the end of the party."

Candy shook her head, her cheeks going pink. "I told you, it's fine," she said. "I can probably wipe most of it off with a napkin."

"But then the stain might set," I said cheerfully. "Really, it's no trouble to run them over to the cleaners. It's the least I can do."

By now Sydney and Akinyi has joined the grow-ing crowd around us. "Go ahead, Candy," Akinyi said, rolling her eyes. "Don't be such a drama queen. Just let her clean the gloves."

"It's really not necessary," Candy said with a frown. "Anyway, the outfit wouldn't be the same without the gloves. I prefer to keep them on."

I shot Bess and George a look. They seemed

confused. For my part, I was getting tired of this game.

"No, really," I said. "I insist."

With that, I reached over and grabbed the edge of one of the gloves. Giving a good yank, I pulled it off her arm.

Candy gasped. So did several of the onlookers. Her whole arm was covered in big, splotchy red patches!

"Oh, wow!" Pandora exclaimed. "What's the matter? Did you hurt yourself?"

"It's nothing," Candy said quickly. "Just, uh, an allergy to some moisturizing cream. I have sensitive skin, you know."

"Yes, just like your fellow redhead Sydney," I put in. "And it looks like those ant bites swelled up just as much as hers did."

"Ant bites?" Sydney looked perplexed as she glanced down at her own carefully covered chest and arms.

"They're not ant bites!" Candy protested.

"Really?" Akinyi grabbed her arm and peered at it. "Hmm, they do look a lot like Syd's bites now that you mention it. But we didn't get anywhere near those ants while they were biting Syd—you were too busy freaking out over how much you hate the creepy-crawlies. So how . . . ?"

"All right, all right!" Candy cried, yanking her

arm free and bursting into tears. "You're right, they're ant bites, okay?" She spun and glared at Sydney. "But I wouldn't have had to do any of this if you hadn't stolen Vic from me!"

"What?" Sydney blurted out.

There were gasps from all around and a flurry of exclamations and questions. But I stayed focused on Candy.

"You're the one who's been sabotaging this wedding all along, aren't you?" I said firmly.

She was crying harder than ever. "I met him first," she sobbed. "He was supposed to end up with me! That's why I *had* that stupid dinner party!"

"Hang on." Akinyi pointed one long finger at Candy. "So if I'm following this, you wanted Vic for yourself—which you never told us, by the way—and so you decided to ruin Syd's wedding by doing all this crazy stuff?"

Candy shrugged and dabbed at her eyes with her remaining glove, clearly trying to regain control of herself. "Well, most of it." She shot a look at Sydney. "It seems like Miss Perfect is having her share of bad luck for once too."

Sydney looked ready to cry herself by now. "Candy, how could you?" she exclaimed.

Meanwhile Bess and George made their way over to me. "Nicely done, Nance," George said as Sydney,

Akinyi, and Candy all started talking at once and Ellie yelled at the cameramen to stop filming. "But how'd you know?"

"Yeah," Bess said. "Last we heard, there was a huge list of suspects and Candy wasn't really even on it."

"I know. Sorry I didn't have time to fill you in, but I didn't want to lose my chance to bust her," I said. "Once those ant bites faded, it would have been a lot harder to prove it was her."

"But how did you know?" George repeated.

Her words happened to fall into a moment of relative quiet. All eyes turned toward me.

"Yes, Nancy." Sydney took a step in my direction. "How did you know it was Candy?"

"It was something Akinyi said a few minutes ago," I explained. "She told that she and Candy were just about the only ones who knew about MrSilhouette."

Most of the onlookers were obviously confused. But Sydney traded a glance with her mother and Akinyi. "Yes?" she prompted.

"That reminded me of something else. The other day Akinyi and Candy helped my friends and me get into the stadium shoot. When we all walked in, Candy looked over at Vic."

Bess gasped. "And Akinyi said something about her always spotting him first!"

Akinyi looked sheepish. "Just a little joke. I sometimes tease her about letting a guy like Vic slip through her fingers. But I swear, I didn't know she actually liked him!"

I nodded. "I didn't think much of the comment at the time, but today it made me wonder if there might be a love triangle going on here." I shot a quick glance at Pandora, who was watching along with everyone else. "One we didn't even know about."

"So who did you call when you borrowed my phone earlier?" George asked.

"The modeling agency," I said. "I wanted to talk to the receptionist who sent out the bridesmaids' dresses. She was off today since it's Saturday, but I convinced the answering service to give me her home number. When I talked to her, she confirmed my hunch—when the dresses came in last week, Candy offered to take the package with Akinyi's dress in it down to the mailroom."

Candy sniffled loudly. "Okay, you caught me," she said heavily. "I switched out my dress with Akinyi's. I knew Kinnie would spaz out and call Sydney when the dress didn't fit."

Akinyi glared at her. "Very nice," she spat out. "You wanted us both to be upset!"

"Right," I said. "So with that prank accounted for—at least circumstantially—most of the rest clicked into place. Candy knew exactly what Sydney's RSVP cards looked like, so I guessed she'd sent that fake one." I shot a look at Candy, who didn't bother to deny it. "She knew that silhouette thing would freak Syd out and could have easily slipped the unmarked gift into the pile."

At that, Candy just shrugged. "I thought that one was pretty clever, actually," she muttered, more to herself than anyone else.

"Of course, she could have contacted the police and the bakery and the flower shop as easily as anyone else," I said. "And sent those threatening e-mails, too."

"Threatening e-mails?" Candy put in. "I didn't send any threatening e-mails. Wait, do you mean that text I just sent?"

Sydney shook her head. "She's talking about those horrible e-mails from last month," she said accusingly. "I can't believe you did that!"

"I don't know what you're talking about," Candy said. "I didn't send any e-mails."

Deciding the e-mails were the least of the issue, I plowed on. "Then there was the hair-gel incident, of course," I said. "Candy was around that day too, so I guessed she'd sneaked in and switched out Vic's gel, then slipped back later and switched them back before anyone thought to check."

Sydney gasped. "You mean you *purposely* let him put that flammable stuff in his hair, knowing the risks?" she cried in horror.

"Get real," Candy snapped. "With all those medics around there was no way he'd really get hurt. I just figured it might scare him a little. Maybe even teach him a lesson about rushing ahead with this wedding."

Shuddering slightly at the idea that anyone could think that way, I continued. "And of course, we can all see that she placed those biting ants, knowing that Sydney had sensitive skin just like her own."

"Yeah. Rotten little things swarmed me while I was trying to get them out of the jar onto that lei," Candy muttered.

I turned to her. "There's still one thing I can't figure out, though," I said. "During the airport party, when did you have time to sneak out and dump that jet fuel in the punch? And how'd you know where to find it, since you'd just arrived in town?"

Sydney gasped, both slim hands flying to her face. "You did *that*?" she cried, sounding on the verge of hysteria as she stared at Candy. "But you could have killed Vic!"

"Yeah, and some of the rest of us, too," Pandora put in.

There was a moment of uproar. "Wait!" Candy yelled over the ruckus. "Listen! I had nothing to do with that, I swear! What, do you think I'm crazy? I definitely didn't want to hurt Vic—I just wanted to show him that his stupid relationship with Syd was moving way too fast!"

Sydney was crying by now. "If you didn't do it, then who did?" she wailed. "That stuff didn't pour itself in there!"

"How should I know?" Candy snapped, clearly on the edge of tears again herself. "Maybe the caterers hate reality TV."

George gritted her teeth, but I nudged her before she could respond. "Let it go," I said softly. "She probably realizes that's the prank that could get her in real trouble. Even if we can't get her to confess, I'm sure the police will take care of it."

"So what did Tonya say?" Bess looked up from scrubbing a tray clean in the soapy sink as I hung up the phone.

It was a few hours later. My friends and I were still at Sydney's parents' house helping clean up after the shower. Deb and Vic's mother were helping too, but the two of them were out in the living room packing up the gifts. Sydney, Ellie, and Akinyi had gone along when the cops had arrived to take Candy down to the police station, and I'd just called in to see what was happening.

"Sydney and the others are on their way home," I reported. "Tonya told me that Candy confessed to most of the stuff, but she still won't admit to the jet fuel thing. Or the e-mails Sydney got back in New York, either."

"Forget the e-mails." George had been drying a pan Bess had just finished washing, but she set it down and hurried toward me. "How are we going to prove she tried to poison Vic?"

I shrugged. "Not sure we can," I said, feeling troubled. "I asked around earlier before everyone left, and it seems like Candy has an alibi for the whole time of the party. She was with Akinyi or Syd or both pretty much the entire time after they disembarked from the jet, though Akinyi did remember her stepping to the back of the plane to make a phone call right after they landed. At the time Candy claimed she was calling their modeling agency, but today she admitted she was actually making that false tip to the police."

"So she has an alibi for most of the party, and then she was outside with Sydney when the PowerUp thing went down?" Bess said.

George looked confused. "So then who did it? Who poisoned the PowerUp? What does this mean?"

Before I could answer, the kitchen door slammed open. Sydney rushed in, face pale and drawn, clutching her PDA.

"Syd!" Bess exclaimed. "Are you all right?"

Sydney didn't answer. She held up the PDA so I could see. "This just came," she blurted out hoarsely. There was a text message blinking on the screen:

R YR FEET GETTING ANY COLDER?

I shook my head grimly and finally answered George's question. "It means this isn't over."